INTENSE DESIRES...

WHEN HORMONES DO THE TALKING...

HANISH BHARDWAJ KHILADY

PHOENIXATE PUBLICATIONS

Ch-1

Start of A Long Friendship...

I was looking for locker number 45 as I walked down the hall of Kendriya Vidyalaya School No. 1 in Vikas Puri, New Delhi. Nishant Tiwari was assigned locker 46. It was directly outside my homeroom, Room 15. For the first time in my life, I knew people on the first day of school. From kindergarten to ninth grade, I attended a different school district every year. It felt fantastic to be back at Kendriya Vidyalaya School No. 1 in Vikas Puri for my second year.

My parents relocated frequently. They moved almost every year I was in school, and they had moved several times before that. By the time we arrived in Vikas Puri, New Delhi, I had already spent time in Pune, Bengaluru, Indore, Udaipur, Ranchi, Lucknow, Ahmedabad, and, yes, Neemrana. For kindergarten, second, third, fifth, and sixth grades, I attended Christian Convent schools.

I am a foodie who enjoys my meals, particularly my lunch. I enjoy decorating it and bringing in a large number of items. My lunch was usually the same every day: two butter sandwiches, one with chicken and the other with egg spread, followed by French fries, an apple, a banana for fruit, and chocolate for dessert. I admire my mother for that. She is aware of my preferences. I went to homeroom after stowing my bookbag and lunch in my locker.

I sat down after seeing my name on the fourth desk in the row near the window, right behind Nishant, of course. Ms. Anita Joshi, a tough-looking, fit, and rigorous lady in her mid-thirties, was at her desk reviewing her homeroom class roster. I knew she'd be teaching introduction to chemistry in 3rd period.

As the last pupils arrived, the bell rang. I knew the majority of those from the middle school where eighth and ninth graders were housed. There were a couple of cute females and a couple of people I'd had issues with the previous year, but no pals. I didn't have many pals. My best buddy from ninth grade had moved over the summer, and my prior best friend, who was still a good friend, lived a few blocks away in Tilak Nagar, near our old house.

The principal came on the speakers and welcomed us, as well as made a few announcements about clubs and sports that had already begun *(the cricket team had been preparing for a few weeks)*, and then we rose and recited the Pledge. This is something I've said every school day, regardless of which school or city I was in. I think I even said it in my nightmares at times. When I get to college, I'm hoping it will go away.

Ms. Joshi called the roll, and when she said 'Ashvani Tyagi,' I answered 'Ashu, Tyagi please,' because that was my code name. She seemed to scribble something in her grade book. This is something I'll be doing every period today. My mother and her relatives were the only ones who called me Ashvani. Oh, and Mrs. Karuna, my ninth-grade English teacher, addressed everyone by their given name. She was a traditional teacher, rough as a coconut on the outside and sweet as a cucumber on the inside. However, I have read that senior secondary teacher can tell by the level of your grammar, spelling, and word choice, how you are going to fare in your life. I had a feeling the rumor was genuine.

Yamini Khanna, a new student from London, England an exchange program student was the really cute barbie in the seat next to me. Little did I know that saying "Hi" to her as the bell rang to send us to the first period would have such a tremendous impact on my life. I could only discern the tiniest accent in her "Hi" back. We exchanged greetings and realized that we had a couple of classes: Math first period and English fifth period. I resolved that this year will be better than the previous one. I was routinely picked on in ninth grade. Being the new kid, being forced to dress differently *(my parents didn't like blue jeans - I didn't even own a pair, and if my parents had their way, I wouldn't till I moved out),* and earning exceptionally outstanding grades made me the focus of a lot of jokes, jostling, and plain bullying. It had gotten better after the class bully challenged me to a fight, which I had accepted. It wasn't even close in the end. I also had bruises on my back and chest on several occasions. Because I constantly asked them to refrain from assaulting my gorgeous face, and they complied by using my body as punchbags. And I always presented myself as a tough guy, acting as though it never hurts when they strike. I'm going to reveal a secret here; please don't tell anyone, it always hurts.

He'd yelled, "Let's go," and taken a swing at me as soon as we were in the locker room. I ducked. But then I swung back. When he dodged, I hit his shoulder, but he was taken aback that I was fighting back. I decided to press it right then and there. I never landed another punch, but he kept backing away, stunned by what was happening. I simply turned around and returned to my locker as the sports teacher entered to check what was going on. Durgesh Saroj never heard the end of it, that he had backed away from someone who was meant to be the class wimp because he had chickened out of the fight. I was aware that I needed to be cautious, but it was close enough to the end of the year that I was able to avoid any potentially harmful circumstances with him. That was the end of the bullying. And I was perplexed as to why I had never attempted it before.

As I walked down the hall to Mr. Ravinder's Health class, I ran across a couple of old foes, including the aforementioned Durgesh. They didn't say anything. Maybe I wasn't supposed to be there. If that's the case, then perhaps, just maybe, 2001 will be a good year for me. I also ran across Priyanka Jha, my ex-girlfriend from the previous year. We had split up throughout the summer, but I wasn't very upset about it. She remained a buddy. An enraged friend used to smack me in the face while laughing like a donkey. Strange! It's bizarre. I'm grateful to her since she ended our relationship, and now I have fewer injuries. He... He... He...

I entered Mr. Ravinder's class, which was only down the hall from my own. My name was on the board, along with a note that said, 'Sit wherever you choose.' I sat in the front row, center, as I had done since I was in elementary school. It made the board easier to view. Yamini sat on my left side without asking, which made me thrilled. A swarthy kid with dark hair and thick-rimmed glasses stood to my right. Just before the bell sounded, he leaned over and said "Ritvik Prakash," and I said "Ashu Tyagi."

Mr. Ravinder took the roll (*'Ashu Tyagi, please,' he observed*), distributed our books and syllabi, and then asked us to introduce ourselves and explain one fascinating fact about ourselves. Each child had a turn standing up and stating their name as well as something noteworthy about themselves. Yamini explained that she had recently relocated from London and gave some background information. Ritvik added that he had a ham radio, and I mentioned that I went to different schools in different cities practically every year.

"What is it?" I inquired.

"Amateur radio, often known as ham radio, is the non-commercial transmission of communications, wireless experimentation, self-training, private recreation, radio-sport, contesting, and emergency communication using radio-frequency spectrum." He concluded.

I was ecstatic to learn about it because I had never used it or even heard of it before. The rest of the day followed a similar pattern. Ritvik and I happened to have the same lunch slot, so we decided to share a table. I mentioned I had a younger brother and sister, and he said he had two younger brothers. Surprisingly, both middle children were named Anoop. His father was a Service Engineer with Infosys, and his mother was a nurse. My father ran a gas station and my mother was a stay-at-home mom. My father's books were done by her, but they were primarily done at home and didn't take long. Ritvik lived too far away to bike from our house in Vikas Puri Blocks, which is a large area in and of itself, but my mother had never refused to give me rides, so I decided we might meet up later.

I inquired if he was a Chess *player (a game I had learned over the Summer from Sourav Bansal who lived just down the street from me, but he was a High School student about to pass out to college).* We both liked chess and played cricket, Ritvik excelled better than me in both games but he never seemed interested, still, he played with me. *'It was the start of a long friendship.'*

Ch-2

A Miraculous Escape...

September 2001

The Indian Cricket Team in 2001, led by Sourav Ganguly, was a team in a rebuilding mode following the fiasco of the Match-Fixing Scandal, which shocked the whole cricketing fraternity, with great cricketing names going down and every game being scrutinized. And India was preparing to meet Australia, the World Champions, in a Three-Match Test Series. They had gone undefeated in the previous fifteen test matches, a world record at the time, and had swept everyone they faced by large majorities. The Australians were the clear favorites, with cricket experts forecasting a 3-0 clean sweep in their favor. I recall the first game of the 2001 series in Mumbai going just as everyone had imagined. Indians were rolled over by Australians. In the second game, Australia batted big 445 all out in the first innings as per India's current form and bowled Indians out for a meagre 171 all out, prompting India to bat again following on.

With the Indians down by 274 runs, the second innings got off to a good start as their first wicket fell for 52 runs. Sadagopan Ramesh was caught at slip by *Shane Warne, the King of Spin (fondly called).* The Indian captain played his gamble by sending VVS Laxman *(also known as Very-Very Special Laxman among his admirers, despite his famous name)* instead of Rahul Dravid, who was out of form and low on confidence. In the previous three completed innings, Laxman was the only batsman in the Indian team who appeared at ease against the Australians. India needed a big score to stay in the match, and he was striking the ball beautifully. The Indians were 232-4 when Ganguly left at 48, down by 40 runs, and another batting collapse could hand the series to Australia, who was sniffing it. Then Rahul Dravid joins Laxman in the center. Laxman was in fine form, and the cricket ball resembled a football to him. Every Australian bowler was smashed by him.

Perhaps, I witnessed the greatest game of Cricket played in my life, perhaps the greatest ever. The marathon collaboration began. Both cricketers brought their A-game, and their onslaught was so intense that Australian captain Steve Waugh was obliged to deploy seven fielders on the boundary, despite the fact that the ball was still crossing it. Dravid had a score of 180, while Laxman had a score of 281, the highest by any Indian for a long time. It was a truly 'Very-Very Special' and a counter-attacking partnership between both batsmen. In the fourth innings of the test match, India declared 657-7 and challenged Australia to chase 384 to win *(2nd for Australians).*

The Australians were particularly heavily hit, and they were still hallucinating as a result of the assault. They were, however, the great Australians. Their openers, Matthew Hayden and Michael Slater, came out firing and put on a show, scoring 74 runs before Harbhajan Singh, dubbed the *'Turbanator,'* got the better of Slater and was caught by Ganguly. Harbhajan Singh put the brakes on the Australians by scoring a hat-trick on the first day itself in 1st innings, at 252-4 Australia was cruising to a monstrous score. The scorecard suddenly changed to 252-7.

In the Harbhajan Singh hat-trick, he first got rid of Australia's rising star back then, Ricky Ponting by trapping him in front of the wicket. Adam Gilchrist was the next one to depart as he was adjudged LBW on the first ball that he faced in the innings and the hat-trick wicket was of Shane Warne, who was caught out. Warne tried to work the ball away only to find Sadagoppan Ramesh at forward short leg, who hung on to the catch. The last decision was referred to the third umpire who decided to give it out, making it the first-ever hat-trick by an Indian in test cricket.

Following that, Australians sank like a nine-pin. The Indians were pleased when they shot Australia all out for 212. What a coincidence, India won by 171 runs, the same number of runs they scored in their first innings. India's victory over Australia marked a remarkable turning point in Indian cricket. It was at this point that self-assurance became apparent. ***It was a Miraculous Escape...*** From there, Indian cricket's graph only moved up as they established themselves as a global force to be reckoned with.

After watching the events unfold during the 5-day cricket match at Eden Gardens in Kolkata, the entire cricketing community was stunned. Even though there were accolades from all around the world, they couldn't believe it. Some referred to it as a fluke, while others predicted that the Australians would come out swinging in the third game in Chennai. The Australian pride had been shattered, and they appeared to be wounded tigers. They had never been as excited to enter a cricket stadium as they had been to enter Chennai. They were eager to put things right as soon as possible. The Indian side was to be demolished. The Series concludes with the third and final game in Chennai.

Waugh and Ganguly both were at mid-pitch for the toss with Match Referee. Waugh correctly predicted the outcome of the coin toss and chose to bat first. In the spinning Indian circumstances, batting first was a fantastic idea. Other than Hayden, who hit a big daddy hundred of 203, only the Waugh brothers, 70 for Mark, 47 for Steve, and Justin Langer 35, scored some substantial runs. The remainder of them only managed single digits, including four ducks *(zero)*, and withered the *'Turbanator Storm'*, as Harbhajan picked up seven out of ten wickets. Australia was all out on 391 till the second day's lunch.

Ramesh and Shiv Sunder Das, India's openers, have now come on to bat. There was a noticeable difference in their stride as they entered the pitch. When they faced Australian and global legends, Glen McGrath and Jason Gillespie, they exuded confidence. With the exception of Sourav Ganguly, who scored 22, everyone in the Indian top six scored at least 61, with Sachin Tendulkar scoring a whopping 126, and India scoring 501. A commanding 110-point lead. Australia batted once more and was knocked out for 264 runs. On the fifth-day minefield pitch, India needed 155 to win the third Test and the series.

India began cautiously, but Das returned a catch to McGrath and the score was 18-1. VVS came in and put together a nice 58-run partnership with Ramesh until a mix-up occurred and Ramesh was run out, with the score 76-2. Gillespie induced an edge from Tendulkar, Jr. Waugh nabbed him at the slips for a score of 101-3. There were millions of Indians hoping for an Indian win as long as Laxman remained on the crease, and 54 more were needed. Ganguly arrived and went, adding 4 to the total, making the score 117-4. Bowled by Gillespie caught by Waugh Jr. Dravid entered, and Kolkata's marathon heroes were on the field. Even when Sachin and Sourav had returned to the pavilion, the Indians remained calm. Collin Miller came in and grabbed three key wickets, breaking the back of India's middle-order at a crucial point in the game, sending Dravid, Laxman, and Sairaj Bahutule back to the pavilion with a score of 135-7. Just in half an hour of play, the Indian team which had been cruising to victory was about to collapse under the pressure.

Sameer Dighe, the Indian wicketkeeper, and Zaheer Khan, the pace spearhead, kept their cool to put up another critical 16-run partnership. Zaheer did not score a single run in the interim, but he also did not lose his wicket. McGrath beat Zaheer when India was only four runs away from the target, and India lost their 8th wicket on 151. Australia was two wickets away from a historic victory, but India only needed four runs to win. The contest was still undecided; it may go anyway. There are nerves all over the place. Not just among the players, but also among the spectators in the stadium, who were watching on television and listening to the radio.

After a few oohs and aahs, the *'Turbanator'* Harbhajan Singh finally tapped the ball for two runs, and millions screamed in joy. I'll never forget that experience. It was like a carnival, with men of many races and religions participating. There are fireworks, candies, and celebrations all over the place. People began to dance on the streets, at offices, and in their homes. Hugs and kisses all around. It wasn't India's victory; it was Cricket's victory. Dada the Leader *(Sourav Ganguly is affectionately referred to by his fans)* was born. True leadership was demonstrated, and one of India's greatest captains declared his arrival in international cricket. 'It was a miraculous escape.'

The academic year was winding down. It wasn't particularly engaging, and the classes were relatively easy thus far. Ajay Kumar's Indian History lesson was the only one that was actually engaging. When matters of a more *"adult"* nature was in issue, he made the lesson entertaining by regaling us with anecdotes that were most definitely not in our textbooks, often remarking "If you want the remainder of that story, you'll have to look it up yourself."

Ritvik and I had both signed up for the same Cricket Training League and requested to play on the same squad. He was improved, but just marginally. Yamini and I had become pals. She had just turned sixteen *(as I would in April of 2002)* and had arrived in New Delhi from London in student exchange program to understand our Indian culture, her roots too belong here. Ritvik and I went to a few of her volleyball games since she was cool. After that, we hung out a few times and discovered that we enjoyed each other's company. Her black hair, blue eyes, and lovely body appealed to me as well.

We didn't have much of a choice for places to hang out near the school, so we mainly sat at shopping malls and sipped soft drinks.

"Delhi is not like London," Yamini explained. "There are coffee shops in all of the big cities, as well as most smaller villages, where we can hang out near the school."

"Vikas Puri isn't exactly a big town - there are a few establishments on H-Block, but they're too far away from school to walk to." Similarly, because you live directly across the street from the school, your mother or mine would have to bring you and Ritvik home."

Ritvik lived approximately two miles from the school and could ride there if the weather was nice.

"What brought you to Delhi?" Om was the one who inquired.

"I had a cousin who traveled to Delhi to study and also performed quite well, and she said it was a lot of fun, getting to know about the real India. So, I decided to come along and give it a shot, even my parents never visited India, as far as I know it was in 1937 when my grandparents moved to England. My parents were supportive and gave me the go-ahead, and here I am. Now it's my job to make my parents proud; they will undoubtedly do so when will explain them about my stay here in India." She explained the whole scenario.

"Do you want to come over to my house, boys? My *'host-mother'*, who is an excellent hostess, assured me that everything would be ok. You may be picked up there by your folks." She invited us.

"Sure!" I said that and walked over to the payphone. I called home and informed my mother that I was hanging out with Ritvik and Yamini at her house with her host-mother, and she promised to pick me up in an hour. I was hoping for a little more time, but she wasn't having it. "Fine," I responded sarcastically, knowing fully well that I'd pay for it when she came to fetch me. But, oh well.

We walked to Yamini's residence, where I met Mrs. Deshpandey, who she referred to as her *"host mother."* She was the same age as my mother and also stayed at home. I believe she knew my mother since I recognized Mrs. Deshpandey from a mutual event with my mother *(my father and Mr. Deshpandey did not attend)* where Ritvik and I were both bored by the constant women's chit-chatty conversation.

We sat on the couch, drinking juices and listening to the radio. Yamini was plainly flirting with Ritvik. He'd just turned seventeen and was rather attractive - certainly more attractive than I was. I could tell she was fascinated by the way she spoke to him, laughed at his ridiculous jokes, and otherwise acted.

Darn. Him. I'm not one of them. Ritvik was either oblivious to the situation, indifferent to it, or both. I couldn't figure it out, and there was no way I could question him right then! I was also irritated that the London angel seemed uninterested in me. I couldn't figure out why we got along so well. Why? I couldn't hold it against Ritvik because we'd become such good friends, but I was envious.

I knew it was time to leave when I noticed my mother's station wagon parked in the driveway. Ritvik requested a ride, and I agreed, knowing that my mother would pick him up. "Man, she's a screamer for you!" A stunning half British half Indian girl! You have to approach her and ask her out!" As we walked out together, I said.

"Nah, I'm not really interested," he responded, looking at me.

"It's insane of you not to ask her."

"Nah, I'm not interested."

I simply shook my head and drove away. It didn't make sense to me. How could he say no to her straightforward offer? What a moron?

"You can't use the tone you used on the phone with me, Ashvani. You're lucky I didn't come to collect you immediately away because I let you come here." My mum remarked.

Nothing came out of my mouth. Whatever I replied would have

been incorrect, and I had learned that if I just kept silent, she would shut up faster. Yes, I had a strained connection with my parents that was only becoming worse. She recognized Ritvik and gave him a warm welcome. He is, after all, a ladies' man. Yamini was previously interested in him, and now my mother is treating him well, as she always does.

"Thank you, Mrs. Tyagi, for driving me home."

"You're welcome, Ritvik," says the mother.

We said our goodbyes to Ritvik and returned home. Dad was home in the early afternoon, as he normally was. He made his own schedule as the proprietor. He loved to get to work early in the morning, come home in the afternoon, and then work in his home office in the evening. My connection with him was far from ideal.

"Ashu, it's time to mow the lawn."

There wasn't even a hello. A typical father. I had an hour before supper, so I figured I'd do it now rather than wait until tomorrow and hear him shout at me for no reason. As I passed by, my brother Anoop put his tongue out at me. I didn't bother to complain because my parents were powerless to intervene. As it was customary.

I changed into shorts and a t-shirt, brought out the lawnmower, checked the gas, filled it up, and cut the grass. Because it wasn't a large lawn, I was able to do it in about 30 minutes, front and back. I didn't have to rake because it was a bagging mower. Before dinner, I had enough time to shower. On my way to my room, I hurriedly showered and passed my younger sister Sheetal.

"Hey, litsy-bitsy," I say.

"Hey, big bro," Sheetal replies in fun.

That's what I'm talking about! She was the only one in the family with whom I got along. She was nine years old, adorable as a button, and quite intelligent. "How is it going with Yamini? Are you going to get anywhere with her?"

"No," I sighed. "Ritvik is more appealing to her. I believe she'll just be a friend with me."

"It's a bummer for you, but Ritvik should be content. He's also adorable!"

"He's not into her!"

"What? Does he have a girlfriend already?"

"Nope. He simply isn't interested. I'm not sure what kind of person he is."

"Well, all the lads in my class think girls are gross," she explained after a brief pause. "Perhaps he still believes that?" She also laughed.

"Maybe. We've never actually discussed it."

We were summoned to dinner by Mom. Chapati and green vegetables It was dry and bland, as expected. She was unable to prepare meals except for my lunch. Dad was a good cook, but he only cooked on Sundays and on the barbecue. At the very least, there was Chicken, so I could eat that and only the bare minimum of greens. The usual mix of admiration for whatever Anoop accomplished, hatred for anything I did, and treating Sheetal like a princess dominated the talk at the table.

Almost everything I said was ignored or despised. The *"Scotch"* event, in my opinion, is a wonderful example of how my parents handled me. "It has to be made in Scotland," I responded in response to my father's remark about Scotch. I'm still not sure why he determined I was incorrect, but he did.

He'd answered, "No, that's not true."

I'd countered, "Yes, it is."

"No, it isn't, and you, young guy, have said enough."

Really? I knew I was correct, so I dashed to the World Book Encyclopaedia's 'S' volume. I also showed him and my mother. And I was immediately confined to my room for a week. I'm not kidding. This happened when I was twelve years old, and I'll never forget it.

I went to bed after dinner and homework and dreamed of Yamini. My terrible luck continued, and she appeared in my dreams, but this time with Ritvik, and she was going to kiss him. Fortunately, I yelled and awoke. I was fortunate enough to have my room, complete with a television and record player, as well as my books. As I lay in bed, I realized that it was just another day like any other. And, I reasoned, there will be a lot more of them this school year. Then I went asleep soundly, this time without having any dreams.

Ch-3

I wanted One, But Wasn't Suffering Without One...

October 2001,

I decided to try something new. JR Journal, the school newspaper, was looking for 10th-grade reporters. I knew I'd obtain my English teacher's approval, so I went to speak with Ms. Gurmeet Kaur, the faculty advisor. She was a high school English teacher who volunteered to cover the junior high newspaper. She requested writing samples, which I sent in the form of a couple of English class essays and my first-quarter history research report on the Colonial Era. She asked a few more questions before promising to get back to me. I was hoping to get in. It would give me something to do after school three days a week. I wouldn't need to return home as early as I usually go. And in some ways, that was a good thing.

A few days later, Ms. Kaur approached me as I was walking to homeroom and informed me that I had been accepted. If I am able, I will attend the meeting that evening; otherwise, I will attend on Monday. My mom agreed to pick me up when I informed her, I might remain after school. When the day's dismissal bell rang, I went to the classroom where all of the layout desks and equipment were set up. Ms. Kaur, along with the rest of the newspaper's "staff," was present. My first task was to write a story about one of my friends, Pradeep Yadav, and his two brothers, all of whom were football players. Alok and Ravi were his younger twins.

Interviewing them and the coaches took roughly a week, as did writing my 600-word story. We were also allowed to make our headlines, and I went with 'The Third Degree.' Yes, it was corny, but that was the JR Journal's way. I turned it in, and it was authorized for publication with my name on the by-line after some minimal editing. Cool. I continued to write pieces, primarily about sports, as it seemed to be my area of expertise.

The Indian cricket team was defeated 3-2 by Australia in a hard-fought one-day series. However, it was a fantastic build-up to the ICC Cricket World Cup in the 50-over format in 2003. New players were arriving and performing. Laxman was picked in the ODI squad based on his test form, and he scored runs and nice runs. The series was determined by the series' last game, which ultimately went to Australia. Sachin made some important runs and a century, but India was still trailing in the middle overs and the Indian death overs bowling was not up to par. Nevertheless, for Indian Captain Ganguly and the entire Indian team, it was a fantastic learning experience. Playing against the greatest helps you become the best. It's not about winning or losing, but about the journey from rookie to legend.

The inter-school volleyball season was in full swing, and I made it a point to attend all of their games in search of stories. Yamini was a fantastic story, so I didn't have to look very hard. After a brief interview with her and a brief conversation with Ms. Joshi, the girls' volleyball team's coach *(of whom I had no prior knowledge),* the story was completed. "A London girl is competing for the position of new volleyball school captain." Ms. Kaur was about to veto it, but when I told her that Yamini approved, she agreed to let me use it. They even featured a photo of her in her volleyball gear. I was allowed to keep the original by our photographer. For the rest of the year, I kept that photo in my notepad.

In November of 2001,

Our school's custodian was about to retire. Ms. Kaur had requested that I write a 300-word piece about him. She thought I should tackle this one because my sports' 'human interest' style had been highly appreciated. They were going to miss the custodian, who had been there for 30 years. I wrote the piece and coined the most famous headline of my brief media career: "You Were, You Are Our Hero, Mr. Shrivastava." Yeah, it's wackier than ever.

Yamini's volleyball season was over, and she now had more free time. After school, Ritvik, Yamini, and I started hanging out at her house. I met Mrs. Deshpandey, her host mother, and Kamini, her "host sister," a seventeen-year-old fox. We had a lot of fun playing hearts, chatting, and just hanging around.

I had a crush on Yamini, but she never indicated that she was interested in me in that way. She'd laugh at my jokes, call me, and hang out with me, but there was never an opportunity to take things further, even to a date-going out with Ritvik in a group was OK, but I don't believe we were ever alone together. And I had the impression it was her doing. Despite my frustration, I didn't press the button. Yamini often talked about her family and friends, but never about a special guy. Maybe it was it, and she just didn't want to admit it.

My father accompanied me to my first cricket match, which I was able to observe in person. Sri Lanka was the opponent for the Indian team. It was a low-scoring match. However, the Indian squad managed to come out on top. When India required 5 runs off the last two balls with two wickets in hand, my heart almost stopped. Yuvraj Singh was on strike and lofted a ball from Chaminda Vaas into the air, but Sanath Jayasuriya caught him inches above the ground at deep midwicket. The next batsman, Zaheer Khan, came on to strike the next ball and despatched the ball into the stands for six runs. Fortunately, my first visit to a cricket stadium resulted in India's victory. I was hoping for additional games. The next time, I'd much rather watch alongside my buddies Ritvik and Yamini.

In December of 2001,

Ritvik, Yamini, and I were at his place on Christmas Eve to exchange gifts. To keep things, cool between us, we had to set a limit. Ritvik got a chess book, and Yamini got a cheap but cute necklace with a "Y" on it and two small pieces of something that looked like diamonds but weren't. Ritvik gave me a collection of comic books, which I adore and have wanted for a long time. Yamini handed me a diary to write in, a personal diary, which was a new experience for me because I was used to writing for the school journal but had never considered writing on my own. Ritvik had the same response from her, and he presented her with a book on Delhi *(detailing the historic events that occurred in Delhi, as well as gorgeous photographs of monuments and some artistic images. I adored that book and was a little envious.)* We had a wonderful time at our own Christmas party.

Christmas, without a doubt, is not one of our festivals, or, more broadly, it is not recognized in our society. However, I spent the majority of my schooling at missionaries' schools. As a result, it simply became a part of us, and we have no idea when it happened. And I'm very sure it has happened to the majority of families in our generation.

My Christmas came and went, and I received a plethora of gifts *(my parents' primary expression of appreciation was the pile of gifts I received at Christmas)*. I spent time with Ritvik and Yamini, played chess at Sourav's house, read, went to the movies, and did everything else a typical fifteen-year-old does. I didn't have a girlfriend at the time, but that didn't worry me. ***"I Wanted One, But I Wasn't Suffering Without One."***

Ch-4

It Was All We Did...

1st of January 2002,

There wasn't any major change in the new year except for the date and month. Working on the paper, playing chess and cricket, and hanging out with Ritvik and Yamini were all on my mind. Ritvik had been working with me on improving my chess skills. My cricketing talents were gradually developing, and I had established myself as a regular in our block squad. In Vikas Puri, a new McDonald's opened, and there, along with it the Movie Theatre, where we used to hang out together. Unfortunately, it's far away from our homes and we usually needed rides to go there. Ritvik was a year older than the other students since he had lost a year of school owing to sickness, but he was still one year away from getting his driver's license. We could generally get a ride thanks to his mother, Yamini's host mother, and my mother.

The first season of a new cricket league began in January and will continue till April. Ritvik and I both joined up, but because the teams were selected at random, we ended ourselves on separate teams this time. I didn't know any of the other members of my team, but they appeared to be kind enough. Yamini came to watch our games on Saturday, and it was always a fun time.

While playing, I attempted to grab her attention, but she seemed uninterested.

Roller skating, on the other hand, piqued her curiosity. She persuaded Ritvik and me to join her on her roller-skating adventure. When I was in fourth grade, I tried it for the first time. I didn't have a lot of luck, and I also didn't have a lot of control. We arrived at the skating rink and hired skates. She was self-sufficient. She was incredible. A London girl on her journey to independence. She appeared different when skating as if she had transformed into someone else. It's as though she was born to do this. She did some incredible tricks with it, and it was very incredible for us. That was something I'd never done before, but it seemed interesting.

Ritvik and I both had a tumble. Quite a bit. But finally, she taught us how to skate, turn, and, most crucially, stop. I wasn't particularly graceful and continued to fall, but I was getting the hang of it. Ritvik, on the other hand, didn't seem to be having much of a good time. He told me that he liked Chess and Cricket over skating, but that he wouldn't tell Yamini since he didn't want her to feel terrible.

We'd had enough *(or, more accurately, my legs and buttocks had enough)* and needed to grab some cold coffee and relax. We sat and spoke, Yamini looking adorable in her pink cardigan, and Ritvik sitting next to her, their shoulders touching. He didn't make much of a response. Because he wasn't communicating, I didn't bring it up with him, but it was evident that Yamini was still interested in him. I sighed quietly while maintaining a cheerful front. I was delighted to spend time with her. I knew she was going in 5 months and that Ritvik would still be there, and I didn't want to jeopardize our friendship or cause him pain, so I simply let it go.

We did make it to a handful of Delhi Ranji Trophy cricket games, but my father was worried they wouldn't make it. In addition, there were not enough fans in the stands.

14th Birthday, April 11, 2002

My birthday was great. My parents showered me with gifts, including a video gaming system that can be readily linked with my room's television. They may have treated me badly, but they did purchase me some nice things. After supper, Sourav, Ritvik, Yamini, and a few other kids from my group were coming over to my house for cake and ice cream. I blew out the candles as my pals finished singing Happy Birthday *(none of us could sing very well)*, wishing Yamini would finally want to go out with me instead of simply being friends. We spent a lot of time together over the last few months and came to know each other extremely well. I knew she was returning to London in some time, so even if my desire came true, it wouldn't last long.

Ritvik surprised me with a new chess set, complete with weighted pieces, felt bottoms, and a great board. Sourav presented me with two new Superman comic book sets. The other members of my group contributed to a Player's Handbook for me, and Yamini surprised me by giving me a mock turtleneck shirt and a pair of blue Jeans. I hadn't told her about it, but she knew my parents would never purchase them for me or allow me to get them. As I held them up and thanked her warmly, I could already see my mother's disapproving expression.

Around 8:30 p.m., Sourav and two of my other pals departed. Because they lived on the same street, they were able to stroll home. Because it was on the way, Ritvik's mother was giving Yamini a lift. We were all waiting for his mother on the front steps of the home. Yamini wished me a happy birthday as she pulled into the driveway, then leaned in and kissed my cheek. I must have turned 12 shades of red. Yes, Priyanka and I had kissed a lot before **(It Was All We Did),** but this cheek kiss was electrifying. "See you at school tomorrow," she said as she walked away with soft lips and a short brush on my shoulder. Ritvik chuckled and remarked, "Man, you're blushing," before punching me in the arm lightly and jumping into the car. They were going after I waved to his mother.

I was ecstatic. I was floating even as mum said sarcastically, "You are not to wear those pants to school." Even my mother couldn't get me down. Was my desire going to come true? And if I did, how would I feel when she went to London in June? A million ideas whirled around in my brain. I had a hard time focusing on my assignment, but I finished it. Then I put the top and jeans on. I looked a couple of years older in that clothing like I was seventeen or eighteen instead of sixteen. And the jeans were comfortable. It was difficult to fall asleep. Yamini's image kept resurfacing in my mind. I grinned and lay down on my bed, gazing up at the roof, seeing Yamini's face, her kiss on my cheek flashing through my mind, and I drifted off to my fantasy - Yamini.

On Wednesday morning, I virtually glided into homeroom. "Hello," I greeted Yamini. "Hello," she said, and I greeted her with a wide smile. I held her hand as we went down the hall after the first-period bell rang *(we weren't in the same class this quarter, but our rooms were adjacent to each other)*. I'd never done anything like this before, and she took a step back. Uh-oh. Is it possible that I misread? We walked to class when I let go of her hand.

I realized after lunch that I had misjudged her. She was well aware of it. It seemed obvious to me. But that was never stated explicitly. For the majority of the day, I sulked. Ritvik was in my last lesson of the day, 8th period. "Man, you got everything you wanted for the rest of your life!"

"No, I don't believe so."

"However, she kissed you."

"As a buddy, yes. There's nothing else. I'm certain of it."

"Did she say that to you?"

"No, but she didn't want to hold my hand, and it was evident that I misunderstood when we ate lunch." "She's simply a pal."

"I'm very sorry, guy."

"Yeah."

For a week, I was depressed, but I managed to keep up appearances with Yamini as I stewed and blamed myself for reading too much into a kiss on the cheek.

In May of 2002,

The first scroll took my breath away... In a galaxy far, far away, after a very long time. Ritvik and I were seated in the PVR Theater, seeing *The Terminator*, a new film starring *Arnold Schwarzenegger*. I was absorbed in the film. When Ritvik and I went to see movies, we typically muttered a little about them, but this one reached out and grabbed us, and we sat in shocked silence. The special effects were incredible, and the plot was incredible as well. We'd see it a couple more times after that. Before then, I'd never seen a movie more than once. I was ecstatic as I walked out of the theatre. It was a once-in-a-lifetime experience.

As usual, the next day, Thursday, I went to Shree Sai Temple for prayers. I normally worked for a month as a Hindu Priest (*Junior*) before taking a month's vacation. My month had been April. I was sitting in with my mother, Anoop, and Sheetal because it was May. Anoop took the corner seat from the right, followed by Sheetal, mum, and finally me. Mrs. Sood was to my left. Her spouse was murdered in the Kargil War with Pakistan roughly three years ago. My maternal uncle was also in Kargil at the same period, but he returned safely. At Shree Sai Temple, I was mostly disconnected from the adult world, although I was aware of the tale because I was a Priest (*Junior*) at Late. Col. Sood's burial. Mrs. Sood and I didn't see one other very much at Temple, maybe every couple of months. Maybe she didn't go anyplace or went to a different Temple most of the time.

I'd been wearing the T-shirt Yamini had given me to Temple since it was so gorgeous and made me appear older. Mrs. Sood lost her position in the prayer book halfway through the prayers, and I assisted her. She couldn't find the proper page for the song later in the service, so I showed her again. "Thank you," she whispered as she clutched my arm. "Thank you, you're really helpful." I simply smiled and returned to my prayers. When the temple rituals were over, I went outside to buy some juice and 'Chole-Kulche.' *(A Very famous dish in Delhi.)*

When Mom arrived, she informed me that Mrs. Sood had asked if I might help her with some yard work, and she had said yes.

"When?" I inquired.

"The next Saturday."

"However, Mom, Yamini's farewell celebration party is on Saturday."

"This is more crucial. Mrs. Sood requires assistance, and you will provide it."

"You don't give a damn about what I want; you never do," I grumbled as I rushed away.

I was lucky that I didn't say it loud enough for Head-Priest Pandey Ji to hear it, otherwise, I would have gotten myself into much more trouble.

I was in a terrible mood on Monday. Yamini figured that out right away immediately.

"What's the matter? You appear to be disturbed."

"On Saturday, Mom is making me do yard labor for Mrs. Sood from Temple."

"Perhaps you could speak with her and see if you could begin extremely early in the morning. Maybe you'll be able to finish in time to attend my party. I'll try my best that we won't start until 4:00 p.m.," she hoped.

"That's something I should've thought of!" This is a fantastic concept. I'll simply sort things out with Mrs. Sood and tell mum she can do anything she wants. I'm sure she'll assist; she appears to be kind."

As a result, a strategy was devised. There is only one issue. I couldn't figure out how to contact her. That night, when

I contacted Ritvik, I described my predicament. He burst out laughing and exclaimed, "Man, you're a moron. Look for her name in the Temple directory. I'm sure her phone number is somewhere in there."

"I'd never considered it. I owe you bigtime, Ritvik."

"What is the point of having friends?" He chukled.

After that call, I felt a lot better. Ritvik, on the other hand, was always able to find the positive side of things!

Without Mom's knowledge, I walked downstairs and took the Temple directory. So far, everything has gone well. Now all I had to do was make sure I could call her without her knowing and then convince Mrs. Sood to go along with my plan. Mom and Dad were both watching TV, so that was a no-brainer. Sheetal was in her room while my brother was out in the yard. I instantly phoned her number from the upstairs extension in my parents' sitting room *(where I made my calls for a bit of privacy).* On the second ring, she answered.

"This is Ashvani from Shri Sai Temple, Mrs. Sood."

"Oh, hello! I wasn't anticipating a call from you. On Friday, I planned to call your mother and give her the timings and facts."

"That's what I wanted to discuss with you. On Saturday afternoon, I'm scheduled to be at a friend's party. She's from London, and this is her farewell celebration. Because of the yard work, Mom won't let me leave." I crossed my fingers in anticipation.

"Oh, my goodness, I had no idea she didn't tell me!"

"She wouldn't," I murmured in disappointment.

"Don't worry, it'll be OK in a week."

"Even if you beg her, Mom would never let that happen. She'll sense something's up, and even if you change the date, she could refuse to let me attend the party."

"Would she do that?"

"It's happened before," I replied very decently to gain some sympathy. "How much work do you have?" I asked.

"Probably around four or five hours." She answered.

"Could I begin at 7:00 a.m.? I know I can't start the mowers or trimmers that early, but I think I could have everything else done by 11:00 a.m.."

"I believe that is feasible. There are weeds to pluck, flowers to plant, chicken wire to put up in the garden to keep the rabbits and stray dogs out, a fence to repair, and finally the lawn to mow. There will be no trimming."

"Can you tell me whether you have a bagging mower?" Is it necessary for me to rake?"

"You've got to rake."

"Could I bring our lawnmower if my father agrees?" It comes with a bag."

"Sure! I'll prepare you lunch, your mother can bring you up at 1:00 p.m., and you'll still be able to attend your friend's party."

"Mrs. Sood, you're cool!" Please don't tell my mother that this was my suggestion."

"Don't be concerned. Everything will be taken care of by me. "See you in the morning on Saturday!"

"Bye, Mrs. Sood," I said.

Boom! Bang on target! I hurriedly hung up and contacted Yamini and Om to inform them of the situation. They were just as ecstatic as I was! All that remained was for Mrs. Sood to phone Mom on Friday and request that I arrive at 7:00 a.m. while concealing the fact that I had called. Fortunately, the Cricket league had just finished the week before; else, the scheme would have failed miserably.

When I went home from school on Friday afternoon, I noticed a note on the fridge that said, "Be at Mrs. Sood's at 7:00 am." I was ready to say "Yes!" when I realized I was meant to be angry about having to go. I went looking for my father.

"Can I borrow our bagging mower tomorrow to Mrs. Sood's?"

"She doesn't have a lawnmower, does she?"

Oh no. How would I know if I had never spoken to her and had not heard from my mother? I had to think quickly.

"Uhm, I'm just worried that she could have one that I don't know how to operate or that isn't in excellent working order."

"Wonderful idea, Son. Who knows now that her spouse is dead? Ok. You're welcome to it. Simply load everything into the station wagon tonight."

Whew! That was a close call. I even received one of Dad's extremely rare compliments.

Dad was a former Air Force Officer who spent over 15 years in the Indian Air Force. He married late in life when he was 36 years old and my mother was 24 years old. Later, I discovered that Dad had never wanted children but had been persuaded to have them by my mother. He didn't want to get married, either. I'm not sure there's a better formula for disaster than this. My father was fifty years old when I was fourteen, so it was like having a cruel grandfather as a parent. My mother's parents, on the other hand, were kind and entertaining. I wished that their parenting abilities had rubbed off on her.

The sun shone brightly on Saturday. I got up at 6:00 a.m., dressed in my Jeans pants *(Yay!),* t-shirt, socks, and sneakers, and walked downstairs to get some cereal, milk, and orange juice, which was my favorite. Yes. I couldn't take the flavor of milk, so I covered it with sugar. I ate my breakfast and awaited Mom's arrival. About 6:45 am she came down with curlers in her hair and a housecoat to drop me off at Mrs. Sood's house. I had a feeling she wouldn't get out of the car!

I cranked up the radio in the car and twisted the dial to listen to some strange sober music so that mum couldn't give me any advice on how to act in public and at other people's houses, among other things. Until we arrived at Mrs. Sood's house, Mom didn't say anything. I was rescued in some way. This was a great way to start the day for me.

"You obey her orders without objecting or arguing. I don't want any accusations that you misbehaved or refused to cooperate. She said I'd pick you up at one o'clock. I'll arrive at 1:15 p.m., giving you plenty of time to get home, shower, and change before I pick you up to drive you to Yamini's. Mrs. Deshpandey will transport you back to our house."

"All right, Mom. I understand. "When she says something, I'll do it."

I jumped out of the car without saying anything else. I knew I'd hear about it, which is why I didn't say goodbye or kiss her. Ugh. I yanked the mower out of the back of the station wagon.

Ch-5

Is That All You Have Accomplished...

I approached the door and rang the doorbell.

As she backed out of the driveway, Mrs. Sood exclaimed, "Hi, Ashvani!" and waved to my mother. "Come over to the garage and let's get this party started." She went back into the house, and the garage door opened. I saw her car, some cans of paint, garden tools, a bike, some weights that looked like they hadn't been used in years, and her mower.

I proceeded to work on the flower garden with the hoe, a little shovel, and a bucket. The huge weeds were plucked and the soil was turned. Mrs. Sood brought several flower-filled pots, and I dug holes next to the path and along the front of the house to plant them. It wasn't difficult labor, and because I was on the west side of the house, the sun didn't shine too brightly.

I completed the flowers at 8:30 a.m. and proceeded to the garage to fetch the fence wire and posts. I walked around the rear of the house and glanced at the garden plot. I could see where the poles had been the previous year; I assumed she had pulled everything down for the winter. I hammered the posts into place with a rubber mallet, then secured the fence wire by wrapping lengths of thin wire around the posts and making sure that the dirt was pushed up against the fence wire. It wouldn't keep a determined rabbit or stray canine out, but it would help. I went to get the hoe and turned over the soil so she could plant it when she was ready after I finished.

Mrs. Sood was standing at the back of the house, watching me work through the sliding glass door. Adults, I assume, don't trust children. I was starting to go into my regular grumpy attitude about grownups, but I resolved not to let it show on her. She didn't know who I was except for the fact that I was a Junior Priest Boy at the temple. It was fine if she just wanted to watch. I'll do my absolute best. I didn't want her to say anything to my mother that would cause me to be late for the party! Mrs. Sood brought out some lemonade after I completed the garden. Because it was in the sunlight, this side of the house was significantly warmer. I was sweating a little, but not excessively.

She remarked, "You're ahead of schedule." I wasn't expecting you to finish things in such a short amount of time. It's too early to start hammering fence planks or mowing the lawn. "Come inside for a while, and we'll get started at 11:00 a.m."

It was just 9:45 a.m. when I looked at the clock. I followed her inside, removing my shoes and placing them on the mat. Her home was spotless. Pictures of a well-built, good-looking, black-haired man in an army uniform hung on the wall. A case with a triangle-folded flag and another case with two medals are on the bookcase. I was certain it was her husband's.

"That was Simarjeet," she replied as she noticed me glancing at the photos. "When he finished boot camp in 1995, we married. After graduating from high school, he enlisted in the army. We dated almost five years before getting married. Any female wouldn't have the courage to refuse his proposition since he was so attractive and determined. But his duties came first, and he was given a week off to be married and travel on our honeymoon. He then embarked on a mission to Kashmir. That was my final encounter with him. I had not expected to be a widow at the age of 24."

I noticed a tear in her eye, but she appeared to be in good spirits. "I apologize for what occurred. My uncle served in Kargil and my father in the Pakistan War in 1971, but they both returned home."

She gave me another glass of lemonade and a seat on the couch. She sat down next to me, and I immediately noted how nice she smelt. I'm sure it was the same perfume she used in the temple since the aroma seemed familiar. She was dressed casually in faded jeans and a t-shirt. Her face was framed by her shoulder-length black hair, and she smiled as I examined her. At sixteen, I wasn't particularly subtle either. She had a fantastic grin, a thin physique, and stunning eyes. Those ideas were banished from my head; she was far too old for me.

"When are you going to graduate?" she inquired.

"Huh?"

"When do you finish high school?"

"Last year," I said hurriedly.

"Wait, you're not seventeen?" she said, her expression darkening.

"No. Last month, I turned sixteen."

"At Temple, I could swear you looked older, but now I see it," she replied after a little pause. "I'm such a knucklehead."

I didn't understand a word she said. The naive sixteen-year-old had grown into a naive eighteen-year-old.

"What exactly do you mean? Are you a knucklehead? Is it possible that I made a mistake? Are you mad with me?" I asked so many questions in her direction.

"It's not you," she answers. She put her head in her hands and said, "I simply thought... never mind."

She was in tears. What the hell is going on here?

"Mrs. Sood, what's the matter? Can I help you?"

"Maybe you can," she murmured as she stared up and deep into my eyes.

"Well, mum said I was expected to help you with everything you needed, and that's exactly what I intend to do. Anything you require." I answered nervously.

Clueless. I was completely oblivious to what I was saying. Or, to be more precise, no awareness of the double entendre in my remarks. I just sat there staring back at her. I was athletic, swam a lot, and had a good muscular tone when I was fifteen. Priyanka had always told me I had wonderful eyes, and I felt I was average-looking. However, I was still in my early teens. I was around two inches taller than she was at 5'5". She got up and walked over to the stereo, where she turned on some light, sober music. She sat next to me and grasped my hand when she returned to take a seat.

"I brought you here with ulterior purposes, Ashvani. I assumed you were older and more attractive. I was also lonely. Now I'm feeling like a fool. Sorry for the inconvenience. It's alright if you want to call your mother and leave early." There were foxy tears in her eyes.

"No," I said, "I'll finish the yard and fence, as well as whatever else you require. It's the very minimum I can do."

"Wow, that's very sweet."

She leaned forward and kissed the inside of my cheek. I reddened a little. A pattern was beginning to emerge. I flush when a gorgeous girl kisses me on the cheek. But this time, I had a different reaction, and my jeans were starting to feel tight. I fought the need to squirm and prayed she wouldn't notice before it passed.

She had taken note. She also laughed. Not an embarrassment-inducing laugh, but a nervous chuckle from someone uncomfortable in the circumstances. She stood up and crossed the room, turning to face me. I just sat there and did all I could to get out of this awkward predicament, but it was futile.

She said, "Do you have a girlfriend?"

"No. Last year, I had one, but we broke up during the summer."

"Sorry."

"It's not a big thing; it was all my fault." I pushed her a little too far to get past kissing."

"Is that all you've accomplished? Just kissing?"

I was now flushed with shame. "Yeah," I confessed sarcastically.

I noticed her standing there, thinking about something. I was terrified of what she could be thinking.

Was she thought of... Nah... Nah... She can't be? What next, if she was...? Does Ashvini agree with that? Let's find it out in the next chapter...

Ch-6

Book Learning and Actual Practice...

I'd seen the parts involved up close and personal before. When I was younger, me and other kids in our area, like everybody else, played "doctor-doctor" and "I'll show you mine if you show me yours" to see what they looked like, albeit not on someone even close to Mrs. Sood's age. As she stood there pondering, all of this ran through my head. She finally returned to the couch and sat down. She asked, "Would you like to kiss me?"

My pulse had to be 140 since my heart jumped into my throat. I was at a loss for what to do next and utterly froze. I couldn't even utter a word. My thing became so difficult that I feared my pants would rip. All I could say was "Uhm, Uhm, Uh."

Mrs. Sood gently turned my head in her hands and kissed me on the lips.

This was electrocution if Yamini's kiss on the cheek had been electric. Every nerve in my body instantaneously alerted me to the fact that a lady had just kissed me. I didn't even return the kiss. All I could do was lean back in my chair and exclaim, "Wow!" She laughed again, this time more gleefully, and took both of my hands in hers. She got up and dragged me up with her. I didn't fight her as she drew me into an embrace and wrapped her arms around my waist. She couldn't have been unaware of my discomfort rubbing against her leg. Her leg was brushing up on my thing! Her breasts pressed on my chest. Her head was resting on my shoulder.

I hugged her back, cautiously wrapping my arms around her. I didn't know what to do or what was happening, but I wasn't going to complain. She became aware of this and broke the hug. We sat across from each other in the kitchen after she took me there.

"Mrs. Sood..." I tried to speak.

"Please call me, Alisha," she says.

"All right, Mrs... Sood... Ali... Alisha. I'm at a loss for what to say or do."

"I see; that's why we're sitting at the table instead of on the sofa. I'd want to speak with you. I'll explain. After that, it's up to you to determine what you want to do. Did you get it?"

"I suppose," I tried hard to figure out.

"Since my spouse died, it's been difficult. I haven't been in the mood to do much. I haven't dated and prefer to stay at home or hang out with my closest high school buddy. I only go to the temple once in a while and spend a lot of time alone there. I assumed you were a senior when I saw you in the Temple, wearing that wonderful shirt, and that you would be graduating soon. You were very kind and gorgeous and well-behaved while you assisted me, and you were so nice and didn't seem frustrated that I couldn't follow the prayer book at all." She explained.

"Your smile was contagious, and your eyes were enchanting. You couldn't be more than 4 years younger than me, I reasoned. I'm not sure why, but something told me we'd get along well. So, playing on the *'widow tale'*, I asked your mother if you could do some yard work for me. I had wanted to bring you over here, but I had no idea how old you were. I made a mistake. I'm sorry I kissed you; you looked frightened out of your mind. I believe I made a significant error. Please accept my apologies." She reasoned with me about the situation and misjudgement on her side. She buried her head in her hands once again.

"Don't apologize, Mrs... oh, Alisha. There was nothing wrong with you. The kiss was one of my favorites. It's simply that I wasn't expecting it. I was completely oblivious to what was going on. You have a lovely figure. You're a wonderful person. You've taken me by surprise, and I'm at a loss for words. I've only kissed a few people before, not as beautiful and ravishing as you are, so this is all new to me. " I was panicking but was trying hard to explain my situation.

"Thank you for mentioning that. It helps me to feel a little better. It's 10:00 a.m., so do the yard work so your mother doesn't become irritated, and allow me some time to ponder. And sometimes for you to relax."

This last bit was said with a hint of humor in her voice. She was, however, correct. I needed to de-stress.

"OK. I'll be finished by 11:00 a.m., with only a few boards to put on and paint and the yard to mow."

I stood up, feeling uneasy from the strain on my trousers, and saw her eyeing me out. Wow, an adult lady kissed me and was inspecting me with her naughty stares, I thought, as I turned and grinned. Would I know what to do if she wanted to do something? Will I be able to make her happy? Would I make a fool of myself?

As I went to get the boards and paint to mend the fence, I attempted to clear my thoughts. The boards were up and the first coat of paint was on in 20 minutes. I started the mower and mowed the front grass fast. I came to a halt to dump the bag before moving on to the backyard. I was relieved that they were both rather little! I emptied the bag one more time, parked the mower in the driveway, and painted the fence a second time. At 10:58, I rinsed the brushes and returned inside.

Alisha had taken a seat on the couch. I was aware that she had been keeping an eye on me. I noticed her at the front window and the rear sliding glass door several times.

"I'm finished with yard maintenance."

"Come in for a bite to eat."

I took off my footwear and walked over to the kitchen table, where I discovered a sandwich, French fries, and a Coke. After working all morning, I was hungry, so I sat down and ate. There was an awkward pause while she ate her lunch. Finally, I decided to speak up. This might be a fantastic day... or a tragic disaster, I knew.

I knew all there was to know about sex, or at least how it worked. My father had made certain that I had several pieces of literature on the topic by the time I was in sixth grade. They were rather detailed in their explanations of the mechanics and difficulties, at least in 6th-grade words. Physical Health class enlightened me a little more on the topic. Fortunately, we had a rather progressive school board, so birth control, STDs, and VD were covered, as well as a review of the mechanics and further anatomical information. However, I was certain that ***"Book Learning and Actual Practical were Poles Apart"***.

"I enjoyed how you kissed me. Quite a bit." I informed her about our brief encounter.

Her face gradually became brighter with a smile. "Would you want another?" she said softly.

Ch-7

Man To Be Soon...

I shook my head and nodded. She stood up, walked around the table, grabbed my hand in hers, and helped me to my feet. I embraced her in my arms and softly kissed her on the lips before hugging her passionately. I was as tough as a rock, and I knew she sensed it. "This can go as far as you want," she remarked as she stepped back and seized both of my hands. You're young, yet something about you, something in your eyes, draws me in like a moth to a flame."

"Are you saying..." I asked.

I didn't answer the question. She took me to her bedroom with a nod of her head. My heart was beating and I was trembling like a leaf. Beyond the material from the books, I had no idea what to do, but she had been married and widowed. She'd be able to tell you exactly what to do. At least, that's what I hoped. It would not be good if I was supposed to know what to do. When we arrived in the bedroom, she locked the door behind us. The queen-sized bed was highlighted by light filtered through the gauze drape. I was dragged into the restroom by Alisha.

"You're dripping wet. Let's get you cleaned up," she dictated to me.

She turned back to me after turning on the water and adjusting the temperature. As I lifted my arms, she tenderly kissed me and grabbed the hem of my t-shirt, pulling it over my head. She placed her hands on my smooth chest and ran them up and down my body a few times before finally halting at my belt. She unbuttoned my jeans, unbuckled my belt, and yanked them down. She took my socks off one by one as I stepped out of my jeans. I was at knife's edge, standing there in my white underpants, in a circumstance I had never been in before.

"Are you sure?" she said as she stood up and looked me in the eyes.

I attempted to say yes, but I couldn't seem to find the words. I agreed, and she reached for the waistband of my underpants, but I backed away just as she was about to pull them down. I chickened out. I pushed her hard and ran away from there.

She tried to stop me many a time, but I just panicked and I didn't want to be there, not right now at least. I hurriedly put on my clothes and shoes and tried to find my socks but didn't see them, so I left them there. She tried to persuade me a lot to be there. Initially, she was requesting, but then her requests turned into screams and threats. The more she talked, the more I drew away from her.

"Ashvani, you can't do this to me? You can't leave me hanging? I'm sorry if I wronged you in any way. I am requesting it from you. I will pay money. A lot of money if you want. " She bragged about many things, offered valuables, and even threatened me. But I didn't stop there.

"Don't worry. I won't be telling anyone this. " And I ran away from there. I knew, somehow, she had made a mistake which she was most afraid of *(What if Ashvani disclosed this to someone? After all, he is just a teenager.)* and I had some part in it, not as equal to her. But being a man **(Man to be Soon!!!),** it is my responsibility that this secret of hers doesn't come out. Otherwise, this society will ruin her life and will make it impossible to live in this world *(Society).*

With my assuring words somehow, she was able to catch her breath and asked- "What should I tell your mom when she comes back to pick you up?"

"Tell her that I left for the party from here," I replied.

"She will be furious that you didn't inform her and go straight up there to the party." She remarked.

"She would be more if we tell....?" I quipped.

I gazed into her eyes, which were not able to match mine. I left from there. Many things erupted inside me. As I was walking down the street to Yamini's house *(which was very far away from here),* I vowed to myself. I would never ever again fall into such a trap. I just escaped a child-abuse instance. Well, I don't consider myself a child, but still, there have been reports of many children around the globe facing the same circumstances *(that we usually read and see on the news).* I never believed such things, but now I believe everything.

Mostly it is considered that child abuse can happen only to females, but no, it can happen to any gender. I wanted to scream and talk to someone about it, but this time it was certainly not the right thing to do. Yes, we were taught *"Good Touch, Bad Touch"* in our school. But I never imagined even in my dreams that such a thing would happen to me. If this could happen to me, it could happen to anybody. I almost reached Ritvik's house but did not go inside. I sat in the park before drinking some cold water from the temple.

My nerves were getting down. I am coming back to normal, but the moments with Alisha flash again. I didn't know how to deal with it, and was trying my best. One thing was running up and down, so that my parents couldn't see me in that state. Obviously, my mother is no less than Detective Vyomkesh Bakshi or Sherlock Holmes. I was more worried than Alisha because maybe I could keep it away from the world, but how could I keep it away from Sherlock Holmes at our home? It was giving me more sweat. Finally, I prayed to Shri Sai and asked him to watch over me and give me the strength that I could keep this secret to myself.

"Now everything is in your hands. If you want me to get punished, then punish me. I always believed, good or bad, that everything happens due to your will. Please don't let anything bad happen to Alisha.. er... Mrs. Sood. Please, Shri Sai, please help me. " I requested. No, I begged.

Ch-8

Military Style...

My mother arrived at 01:30 p.m. at Mrs. Sood's house and chatted briefly with Alisha, i.e., Mrs. Sood *(who was not matching eyes directly with my mother)*. My mother quizzed her about why I had gone so early. Mrs. Sood provided explanations, but my mother remained unsatisfied *(I told you she was the Lady Sherlock)*. My mother inspected the entire house and garden yard and discovered that everything was in order and that I had completed my allotted tasks flawlessly. She was in the midst of a life-changing experience *(or what you call it—shell-shocked)*. Mrs. Sood offered my mother money in exchange for my services *(gardening, not anything else, crazy minds!),* but she rejected them. My mother explained to Mrs. Sood that it was our way of assisting those in need and that money would destroy the kid's life.

"Hopefully you people stick to the same philosophy, otherwise I almost ruined your son." Mrs. Sood murmured to herself.

"Did you say anything?" Mom inquired.

"Yeah! You did a fantastic job raising him. He is well-mannered, behaves extremely well, and is conscientious about his work. I hope and pray to Shri Sai that the child will get all the love in the world and have all of his wishes fulfilled. " Mrs. Sood put on a brave front and complimented my mother on my upbringing.

Mrs. Sood managed to trick my mother by complimenting her on my upbringing, something no one had ever done before, and no one ever wanted me in their house or around. Once, Mrs. Khatri asked me to her daughter's birthday celebration when I was ten years old. Mrs. Khatri wears a wig, which I discovered accidentally. She bent down a bit with her daughter to cut the cake *(I was standing just next to them).* I grabbed her wig and went down the street, followed by all the other kids, and we all played with it by flinging it about.

Meanwhile, at Khatri's residence, Mrs. Khatri and her daughter dove headfirst into the cake. After that, everyone in our neighborhood was terrified of my mischievous character, and I was never invited to another home party *(except for Yamini's House Party, which may not have known much about me; Prince Ashvini gets the benefit of the doubt).* But believe me when I say that I have no idea how such things happen to me. I can't stay in one spot for long. But it was when I was a kid, and stuff like that is intended to happen when children are around. Even though I'm a 16-year-old hunk *(mature enough),* let alone girls, even women are mad about me *(Remember! Mrs. Sood!).*

My mother's eyes welled up with tears when she learned about my indiscretions. It was the first time someone had complimented me. "Thank you so much, Mrs. Sood! If you ever want his services again, please contact me and he would be happy to assist you. " My mother responded by grasping both of Mrs. Sood's hands.

"Mrs. Tyagi, without a doubt." Mrs. Sood replied with a phony grin.

My mother had forgotten why she had come, didn't ask many questions, got into her car, waved at Mrs. Sood, and went directly to our house.

I arrived at the party on time and was floating as I stepped in. I came to my senses when my mother called Mrs. Deshpandey's at 3 p.m. to see whether I had arrived safely. Mrs. Deshpandey handed me the phone, and for the first time in my life, I sensed joy in her voice as she told me she was proud of me.

"If you ever found out the truth, you'd murder her *(Mrs. Sood),*" I murmured.

"Did you say anything?" Mom inquired.

"No, mum, there has to be some sort of inter-connection on the phone." I stood up for myself.

OK, don't worry about that; just enjoy your party and go home on time. I was enraged when Mrs. Sood informed me that you had gone to Yamini's house without alerting me, but her praise for you compensated more than for the disobedience. But bear in mind that you'll never do it again. "Got it." Mom felt she had gone too far in my praise and I had to keep grounded and decided to end it in her unique way *(Military Style).*

"Of course, mama! I'll never do that again. " I then hung up.

I'd never felt so good in my whole life. It had been a fantastic day *(except for a few things that just went overboard).* Yamini began to give me odd looks after approximately an hour. I assumed it was due to her impending return to London, but I didn't give much thought to it. I basically drank my Coke, ate my meal, talked to Ritvik, Yamini, and a few other gorgeous females from my class, and had a fantastic night overall.

At 8:00 p.m., Mrs. Deshpandey offered to drive us back to our respective homes. My parents were unable to pick me up since they were out for the evening. They had a date night on Thursday, but today they were going to see a performance. When I got home, Preeti, one of the neighbors' daughters, was with Anoop and Sheetal. She stepped out the door as I walked in.

I hadn't even taken off my shoes when the phone rang. I responded.

"Hello."

"Ashvani, this is Yamini. What happened to you before you came to my house today?"

"What?"

"An event occurred. You were different; you were less shy and a loser but more self-assured. You even spoke with Aanchal Gupta! Who was she? " Yamini wondered.

I had a crush on Aanchal Gupta, a cheerleader, since ninth grade, but she was way out of my league.

"What?"

"I'm aware of the reason behind the change. Are you going to tell me how it went?" she asks.

"No. You are correct. That did happen, but I'm not sure what happened. She'd never be with me again if the girl found out I told you."

"Wow," she said with a giggle. "I'm from London, and you've done something I haven't. We have a good name to keep!"

It was a running joke between us (*guys*) about London females being easy to catch. She argued that the only difference was that English people were more outspoken about it. That had always sounded more my pace than the conservative Delhiites, but I didn't believe I'd ever get the chance to find out.

"You know, I'd be delighted to help you with that problem."

I suppose being with Alisha has given me a new sense of self-assurance. That was something my friend had observed.

"Well, see you in class on Monday," she chuckled again.

"Bye."

I hung up the phone.

Around 10:00 p.m., the phone rang again. We didn't generally get calls so late, so it was strange. I assumed it was Mom and Dad calling to let me know they were running late. It was, to my surprise, my grandma. She jumped right in. "Where are your parents tonight, Ashvini?"

"They went out tonight instead of Thursday this week," I replied hurriedly.

"Yes. But where have they gone? I must know!" Grandma inquired.

Her tone seemed strange. "Let me have a look at the calendar," she said. It appears that they had tickets to a movie in a South Delhi theatre. They made no mention of a change of intention. Why?"

"Thank God, thank goodness. I was concerned they'd gone to Green Park's Uphaar Cinema, which they aren't *(it was one of their favorite movie theatres)*." Grandma shows some relaxing tone.

"Why?"

"Turn on the television. I'm going to have to call my other kids. " She hung up the phone.

I tuned in to the news station to hear the newscaster. On the screen, there was a large fire raging. My parents go to the theatre at least once a month. When a fire broke out, 59 people perished and another 103 were badly injured. When the whole extent of the tragedy was revealed, it was evident that my parents would have been right at the center of the worst portion of it. That was a strange sensation.

Fortunately, they weren't present there, and it was swiftly forgotten by a sixteen-year-old, because I was preoccupied with something else in my life which I had never imagined. I was going to retire to my bedroom for the night, but sleep was eluding me.

I had memories of Alisha, Yamini, and Aanchal the entire night. They all arrived in turn, and I fell asleep at 4 or 5 a.m.

Ch-9

To Become A Eunuch...

In May of 2002,

On Monday, I saw Yamini in the school canteen and just smiled as she walked past me to take her seat. She giggled and swatted me on the shoulder, saying, "Oh stop."

It was a happy time. As I walked down the corridor, I began to see girls at school in a different way. Girls didn't terrify me as much anymore, and I had a new sense of self-assurance. They intrigued me and fascinated me. And I wanted more of what I'd had with Alisha, albeit not with her, but with other females of my age. It was clear that the kissing I'd had with Priyanka wasn't going to cut it.

There were only three weeks of school left, and only five weeks till Yamini had to return to London. I will be starting a summer camp class provided by the school's "Numerology" department a week after school concludes for the year. I hoped to be accepted into the program my freshman year, and I believed that this would give me an advantage. After that lesson, I'd be returning to Camp Nanital in Uttarakhand (*it was previously part of Uttar Pradesh State, but on November 9, 2000, it became the Republic of India's 27th state*) as I had done for the previous two years.

The two weeks seemed to drag on forever. Almost every day, Yamini torments me with her attractive and seductive Rahul remarks. He was a senior in our school, and most of the girls liked him after seeing the comedy-drama movie *Kuch-Kuch Hota Hai,* in which the hero was named Rahul. Ritvik wasn't much better; I believe she whispered something to him, but I had no way of knowing for sure and wasn't about to inquire. I didn't want anyone to figure out who it was or for the information to spread. I expected he'd bring it up soon, and I'd have to figure out how to respond to my closest buddy.

During those two weeks, Mrs. Sood spoke with my mother on the phone several times, the majority of the time when my mother contacted her. If she needed anything, I was willing to assist her; my mother had volunteered my services several times. Mrs. Sood was a cunning fox who made it difficult for my mother to trap her. She played hard to catch. The more my mum offered, the more she refused. Then she requested my services on a Saturday morning, which my mother agreed to. She told me that I had to assist her in whatever way I could.

"She only wants one thing from me? Me." I talked to myself.

"Did you comment? What does she want from you?" While cutting vegetables in the kitchen, my mother asked a question. This time, she does hear. Sherlock has returned.

"I mean, she's got to need some more gardening and planting. What else is there? " I attempted to mask my anxieties by answering while moving away from the kitchen and my mother to the TV room.

"You didn't seem quite right to me. There is something odd about your tone. Is everything going well for you? " My mother followed me to the TV room, and her detective antennae were spot on.

My throat had dried up, my taste had faded, my mind was blank, and I was at a loss for words. "No... No... I'm perfectly fine. Maybe it was a crazy day in school, and I had to stay afterward for journals. *(Which, of course, I hadn't; I lied.)* That's probably why I'm weary; a good night's sleep could help. " I grabbed my luggage and dashed upstairs to my room.

"Stop." She ordered.

I froze at the top of the steps. "Yes, you're correct, it may be due to exhaustion," she responded, after checking my temperature *(by placing her palm on my forehead).* "I hope you've eaten; if not, remain for another 10 minutes and I'll fetch you a nice supper and soup, and I'll make sure you have a good night's sleep."

"No, mama, I've eaten at school *(no, I haven't)*." I lied again because I was afraid that if I remained two more minutes, my mother would get the better of me, and 10 minutes seemed like a lifetime.

"All right, then get some rest, and yes, you have to be at Mrs. Sood's house by 7 a.m. tomorrow." She made her way back to her kitchen.

I huffed and puffed my way into the room, taking a deep breath. Mrs. Sood was a huntress, and she was staring at me. I was her target, and she wasn't going down without a fight. Let's see what occurs tomorrow; for now, I'd want to unwind. I'll have to think of a clever way to cope with this scenario. If any of my actions with Mrs. Sood were to be revealed to my mother, she would be devastated, and only God knows what she could do. *(She isn't a quitter, but she is capable of murdering Mrs. Sood.)*

Saturday arrived, and I was able to get my bike out of the garage. I was leaving early, so I left a note for Mom on the refrigerator, explaining that I was going to visit Mrs. Sood and would be back before supper. I mounted my bicycle and began pedaling down the street. At 7:00 a.m., I took the shortcut through the tight streets, got back on the road, and arrived at Alisha's house.

Alisha answered the door when I knocked. She smiled at me while wearing a robe. She let me in and closed the door behind me. She drew me into an embrace and kissed me as soon as it was closed. She took a step back and invited me into the living room, asking how I was doing. Rather than sit on the couch, she sat in a plush chair.

"I want to chat to you, but I don't believe we'll get anything done if I sit next to you!"

I sat down on the couch with a smile.

"Two weeks ago, something incredible happened. It's something I'd want to see happen again. But you're so young and should be with females your age, and I need someone with whom I can have a relationship. When you departed the last time, I felt like a weight had been lifted off my shoulders, and I could breathe again. "

She noticed my melancholy, realized I was about to say something, put her finger on my lips, and went on.

"Don't be upset! I'm not going to send you away. Not today, at least. But I'd like you to know that whenever I meet someone, it needs to come to an end. And if someone suspects anything, it needs to stop. If we're detected, I won't go to jail, but my reputation will be wrecked, and I'll have significant issues. And you may as well. So, let's make the most of it while it lasts. " She offered her terms.

As I told you, she won't go down without a fight. See how she was manipulating me.

"Alisha," I added, "you are a lovely lady, and no one would dare pass up such a chance with you. And you know, the last time I was in this situation, I panicked. I'd never done anything like that before. Who knows what might have happened if I had been eighteen years old or older? But, because I'm not 18, and you're not a minor, my conscience won't let me go any further. I know I was at fault the previous time, and leaving you in such a situation was the worst crime any man could commit *(in the Mahabharata, Arjuna was cursed by Urvashi to become an eunuch for life, but Indra intervened and lowered the punishment to "one" year. During the 13th year of his exile, when he was obliged to disguise his identity, Arjuna employed this curse)*. But I still have two more years to grow into a man, so you have my friendship. I would visit your home on a weekly or biweekly basis. We'll play games, listen to music, watch movies, tell stories, and do anything else you like. " I attempted to persuade her to see my point of view and make amends.

"Can I have everything I want, hun?" She inquired with a naughty raise of her eyebrows.

"Except that, you may do whatever you want."

"Friends?" She extended her hand to shake mine.

We exchanged handshakes, and everything appeared to be good for the time being.

Ch-10

Never Say Never...

"I thought you were too young, but I let my passion get the best of me," she added after a glance at me. "I realized right away, Ashvini, that this could never be permanent. I assume you're wiser than I am. You may not realize it right now, but you will. So, let's just take it easy and enjoy our relationship. You'll meet someone your age and then move on. You're a sweetie."

I sulked.

"We still can't be seen together in public, we can't go out," she said softly. "And you're well aware that sex isn't a relationship *(obviously it's off the table now for us).* If we need to end this right now, I'll do so. However, you must accept the truth of the circumstances as well. You gave your friendship, but you couldn't announce it to the rest of the world. Nobody will be able to comprehend the essence of our friendship," she explained.

I thought about what she said. I knew she was right. It did not appeal to me. It was a difficult lesson, but I resolved right then and there not to be hung up on 'S-E-X'. It was a turning point that would bring a lot of joy, but also a lot of heartache.

"Someday, as I said, you'll find the person who is perfect for you, who you can take out on dates with, be seen with, and not have to sneak about with," she continued as I stood there contemplating. "I understand your sadness, but it will pass, and I believe you will remember this fondly."

She was probably correct on both counts. I couldn't help but shrug and answer, "I guess."

"When you grin, you look a lot better. You'll have those females drooling over you because of your grin and eyes. And you don't want me to add to the confusion if you do meet someone. She'll almost certainly want you solely, and you should be aware of this. The majority of women will refuse to share their boyfriends *(The Man)* with another woman. And you should always honor your promise and consider this to be the most important thing you've ever learned. "

Alisha's counsel is excellent. Although it was a different story when it came to obeying.

She then offered me orange juice, which I accepted, and went outside to weed the flowerbed while she began planting seeds and little plants in her garden. It was late enough when I finished the wedding that the mower wouldn't wake the neighbors. Alisha was raking the grass as I was cutting it *(her mower didn't have a bag, after all).*

I rushed into the shower to wash the sweat and grass off my body while she prepared lunch. She stopped short and remarked, "That was Simarjeet's..." as I stepped out wearing a terry cloth robe, I discovered on a bathroom hook *(my clothes were filthy, dirty, and grass-stained).*

Oh, no. I should have given it some thought. I quickly turned around to remove it.

"Ashvini, come to a halt. It's all right. I've accepted that he's gone. Seeing you in the robe was a pleasant surprise, though. "

I felt a lot better. "Well, I could still take it off," I said as I pulled the knot back gently.

"Stop it and take a seat. I'll take a brief shower and then return."

I sat down at the kitchen table, looking at the same meal as the last time - sandwiches, chips, and cokes. She returned in less than 5 minutes, still dressed in the same robe she had worn that morning *(the previous one).* We had a good time eating and chatting. She inquired about my school and acquaintances. I assured her that my school was fine, with mostly A's and a few B's for the year.

"However, there is an issue with my pals. I only have two decent ones, and one of them is departing in a few weeks."

"Who's moving out?"

"No, I don't mean that. Yes, she'll be returning home."

"She?" Alisha inquired, a glint in her eye.

"I wish", I groaned and spoke. "However, at the start of the year, she had a crush on my friend Ritvik, who is the other priest boy with me on Thursdays at the Temple. For some reason I don't understand, he seemed uninterested. And she and I never progressed beyond being friends. And now she's returning to London," I lamented. "I'm not sure I'll ever see her again."

"Never say 'Never.' You have no idea what will happen? Maintain contact with her. Write to her regularly. You never know what life has in store for you. I certainly didn't expect to be a widow at the age of twenty-four. I feel so wicked!" she exclaimed with a gleam in her eye, then smiled, "or to have taken a sixteen-year-old priest boy almost to bed!"

I simply grinned. I didn't know what to say at that time.

"Can you tell me where she's from?" Alisha had inquired.

"London! I don't know how many times I have to tell you."

Alisha burst out laughing. "Let me get this straight: you were rejected by a London girl. Did that teach you anything?"

"Yeah. Girls in London aren't 'easy.' Yamini and I have a running joke about it. When I try to progress beyond just being friends, she shifts the conversation, ignores the comments, or somehow deflects it."

"Did you ever imagine that she's thinking the same thing you're thinking - that she's leaving and may never see you again?"

"No, Ritvik piqued her curiosity. She even admitted it to me. It's probably just me."

"Don't be too certain. You stated that happened at the start of the year?" She is trying to raise some hope in me.

"Yeah."

"Did you ever try to get things along?"

"It was my birthday in April. I felt an electrifying thrill as she kissed me on the cheek."

Alisha burst out laughing once again.

"Boys!" she said, exasperated. "Of course, men aren't any better. If you pay attention to them, they will follow you around like puppy dogs! Consider this: it was the month of April. She'll be back in the first week of June. Do you think that made a difference?"

I came to a halt to consider it. "Yeah, it could have," I said slowly.

"Then give her a break. She appears to be a nice girl. And you never know what may happen in the future. Simarjeet and I met in Middle School and remained friends until we graduated from

High School and married after five long and eventful years of dating."

"Yeah, she's a good friend. She figured out that I did something extravagant on that particular day, without me saying a word to her!"

"What?" Her voice was trembling with surprise.

"She won't say anything to anyone. Well, maybe to Ritvik, but he's not going to say anything, I'm sure. He's too good a friend."

I could even see that Alisha was anxious.

"What exactly do you mean when you say she's figured it out?"

"She glanced at me and observed me as I went to the party *(Obviously hers)*. She called me that night, shortly after I came home, and inquired who I had been with. She inquired as to what had occurred before I arrived at her residence. She claimed she saw I was becoming more confident and that I had spoken to a girl for whom I'd had a hidden crush all year-a cheerleader. Then she asked, plainly, "Who was she?" I pondered for a few moments before admitting that it had happened and that I would never reveal who it was, since I didn't want it to be known that I would kiss and tell. She's been mocking me for the past two weeks about how I'm not a virgin while she is. And this after all of our mocking about London females being easy, "I explained.

"OK," Alisha murmured, after a little period of relaxation. "That doesn't appear to be a bad idea. But don't you see why we can't continue to see each other as friends now? It's quite risky. This adds to the excitement, but it also raises the risk of calamity."

"Yeah, I guess I see that," I groaned.

Today, we spoke a lot. Yes, a lot. It was a whole new experience for me. I learned a great deal about her. She is a cunning fox, but she is also more intellectual. Her words are always logical and magical simultaneously. Her knowledge of a wide range of topics is unsurpassed. If you give her a topic, she can talk about it for hours. I had a great time listening to her. I could call her my life's love, but I'll never be able to have her. Now I'm thinking about how most love-story movies end with couples being separated.

I kissed her *(on the forehead)* and held her before taking my last shower of the day. She remained on the couch, thoroughly satisfied and smiling. I got dressed quickly, stepped over to the couch, kissed her on the cheek, and quietly murmured, "Bye."

"Goodbye, Ashvini," she whispered, tears streaming down her cheeks as she gazed at me.

I went out, got on my bike, and rode slowly home, thinking about all that had happened and dealing with the whirlwind of emotions. I knew I'd see her again, but I also knew that the previous two weeks would have a special place in my heart for the rest of my life.

Ch-11

Don't Disclose This To Anyone...

June 2002,

I went straight to my room after getting home and grabbed a Coke and some chips. I didn't believe I'd be able to handle my parents, Anoop, or Sheetal. I just needed some alone time. That wouldn't surprise anyone because I used to read in my room all the time. In addition, I now have the television that my mother gave me for my birthday. I changed the channel to National Geographic and read while watching episodes of 'The Beast in the Woods'. I needed to clear my head in preparation for my final examinations, which began on Monday.

We visited Shri Sai Temple on Thursday. "Hello, Mrs. Sood," I said to Alisha as we passed the temple.

"Hello, Ashvini!" she said with a smile. After that, she headed to her seat.

"Mrs. Sood phoned yesterday to say you did a terrific job and she was appreciative of all you did," my mother remarked. "I offered your help to her throughout the summer, but *she (Mrs. Sood)* didn't believe she would need it."

I replied, "All right, Mom," but I was surprised.

I felt dead set on not letting anything show. I sat down and glanced two rows ahead. Alisha was seated next to a young man of her age. Throughout the prayer, I was thinking about that. Because my mind was creating all kinds of wicked notions, I don't remember what the topic of prayer was. The words merely flowed around me, barely registering in my mind.

I noticed Alisha flirting with the guy she had been sitting next to after prayer. I just went to the vehicle for the journey home, clenching my teeth, and knew it had to happen. It was going to be another day of attempting to cleanse my mind and organize my ideas.

I walked to my room, turned on the radio, and took out my history book to study for my test on Monday. History was my favorite topic, yet it was difficult at first. That's why I started with it. I got lost in the post-Civil War era of America, going over presidential elections, Indian policy, and the build-up to the Spanish-American War.

I'd calmed down and gotten my emotions under control enough

by Monday that I thought the exams would go smoothly. Yamini and Ritvik, as well as Priyanka *(my 9th-grade lover)* and Shivam Narayan, her new boyfriend, joined me for lunch. We were all quite decent students, so we didn't have anything to worry about with examinations, so we spoke freely.

Priyanka had the most difficult time, as she was in the concert band and had to perform a solo piece as part of her final test. We discussed the upcoming class party at Lalit Jha's residence on Friday night. Lalit's family resided in a renovated farmhouse with a barn large enough to accommodate the full eighth-grade class, even if everyone came up. *(as well as students from other institutions).*

We broke off after our lunch break to go to our tests. I'd finished my English exam earlier in the day *(nothing to study there - I was an ace thanks to Mrs. Suman Jamwal).* The test papers were given out by Mr. Ajay Yadav. As I expected, there would be ten multiple-choice questions, ten true/false questions, ten fill-in-the-blank questions, and two essay questions.

I completed about half the time allocated for the test and still had a lot of time to review. On re-reading one T/F question, I recognized it was a subtle trick, so I revised my response. Mr. Ajay Yadav is Mr. Ajay Yadav. I double-checked all of the questions to be sure I hadn't made the same error. Nope. I figured I'd get an A if he liked my essay responses, and that I could even have aced it.

I didn't think the essays were a problem, my term paper in November had been on- Shri Sardar Patel. I titled it- **The Ironman of India** and wrote that it was *"A Deserving Person Who Missed the Opportunity to be Indian Prime Minister, as Per Indian Politics, still United the Nation."* I had an A+ on that paper and the highest praise from Mr. Ajay Yadav in his comments. *(I still have a copy of that paper to this day; too bad the country didn't figure out what I had).* I was in a good mood. But I knew it wouldn't last long. Tomorrow was Sanskrit with my arch-nemesis in this world, Mrs. Poonam Singh.

Mrs. Poonam Singh, dubbed *"Miss Bubbly"* by the pupils due to her similarity to the popular TV character, seemed to despise everyone, but she seemed to have a grudge against the boys in the class. *'Rule #1: The Instructor is Always Right; Rule #2: If you think the teacher is in error, go to rule #1,'* That was her philosophy. And she meant it.

In 9th grade, I had the most awesome language teacher for Sanskrit. In 10th grade, I had the worst. I dreaded having her for another year, but I wasn't ready to bail on Sanskrit just yet. After all, I had started before-school Sanskrit classes in 6th grade when we lived in Nagpur. That was in the late 90s, just around the Kargil War and India's Nuclear Test at Pokhran, Rajasthan, under the awesome leadership of our Prime Minister, Shri Atal Bihari Vajpayee, and we succeeded in both. We won the Kargil war and there were some great rumors regarding our Prime Minister at that time. One of them was that America's political representative called the Indian Prime Minister to warn and bear the consequences if the war continued against Pakistan. The American representative said, *"Half of the Indian Republic will be doomed by the morning if India doesn't step back from the war."*

The Indian Prime Minister replied, *"I agree. But I also assure you, the whole of Pakistan will vanish from the world's map by the same morning. We didn't start the war, but yes, we shall be the ones to conclude it for forever. "*

The confidence and determination in our Prime Minister's voice changed the perspective of the American representative and the rest is history. This was the beginning of a New India in the making, and it all started with Mr. Vajpayee's era. And people like our honourable Prime Minister, who have contributed a lot and played a significant role in the making of a nation, make me love the subject of history more. Such instances give me chills, and the craving to know more always excites me.

I'd planned to go home tonight and catch up on my reading. I'd be learning verb conjugations, reviewing vocabulary, taking practice exams from a Sanskrit book I bought myself, and going through all of the homework activities. I wasn't sure it would be enough. I only wanted to get a B in Sanskrit by scoring well enough. I had done so for the previous three quarters, but only just managed to get the passing points in each one. It was also a close call on this one. This time around, I'm a lot more focused.

It wasn't that I didn't understand the topic, didn't complete my assignments, or performed poorly on tests. No, Mrs. Poonam Singh graded us on classroom involvement and oral language abilities for 25% of our grades. And I had no reservations in stating that she preferred females and gave boys terrible grades. My *'participation'* scores were low enough that if I didn't obtain a 75 in the final, I'd receive a 'C.' I thought, I could accomplish it, but it would be difficult. She made the examinations challenging and was always able to discover anything I hadn't gone through, thoroughly enough. I'd promised myself that this time would not be one of them.

At 12:30 a.m., I finally closed the books. I didn't have to get up until 6:30 a.m., so I had plenty of time to sleep. Fortunately, that day's Sanskrit test was the only one I'd have. I did have the *"Physical Test,"* but I was able to pass it while sleeping and even with a fever. The sit-ups, push-ups, and running standards were simple to meet, and because the test was pass/fail, I just needed to meet the bare minimum to pass. It's simple enough. On the bright side, I was able to see my adorable classmates dressed in shorts and t-shirts. Bonus!

Tuesday dawned rainy and cool, and I trudged to the bus stop with my umbrella up. Not an auspicious way to start the day. I sat next to Preeti Baghel on the bus. She lived next door and was a tomboy of tomboys. We talked about sports; she was hell crazy about sports. Cricket, badminton, football, tennis, wrestling, any sport, you just name it and she will update you about each aspect of the game. The players, the history of the game, the rules, anything. She was a living encyclopaedia of the sports world. And she excelled on the field as well. Once, she was challenged by our class champion, Shivam *(Priyanka's boyfriend)* in a 100m sprint, and she beat him by a great margin. Fortunately, I was on the tracks that day, and what every one of us witnessed was just out of this world. As the race started, she just didn't run, it was like she flew from there. Hats off to the girl, and I developed a crush on her on that day *(Don't disclose this to Anyone)*.

When we arrived at school, the rain had subsided to the point that I didn't need to use my umbrella to go from the bus to the building. I headed to the classroom after dumping my belongings in my locker. The bell sounded, and I went halfway across the building to Mrs. Poonam Singh's class after regular practice. Pawan wasn't in this class; thus, the first seat was near the window *(it was an alphabetical seat order kind)*. I sat down, placed my two pencils and eraser on my desk as she had requested, double-checked that no one had left any additional papers or anything on or beneath the desk, and waited.

She walked in with a smug expression on her face and gave out the exam papers without saying anything. I selected one and returned the stack to Shivam Narayan, who sat behind me. Of course, the papers should be placed face down. She yelled "Begin" after everyone had their papers and then sat down at her desk to keep an eye on us like a hawk on mice. I flipped over my page, dropped my head, and began reading.

I'd developed a habit that followed me well throughout my academic career *(at least when I followed it)*. Before I even signed my name on the paper, I read the full exam *(all three pages)*. I grew increasingly happy as I read each question. There was nothing I didn't know. I reached the bottom half of the last page, where her customary surprise awaited me. I cocked my head and smirked. I'd guessed correctly.

I had double-checked that I had learned all of the verbs, paying extra attention to several irregular ones we had just briefly discussed in class or used in assignments. I went back to the first page of the test and began working my way through it.

I completed doing a fast review and discovered a few spelling problems as well as an accent that was missing. When she gathered the papers, I knew I'd gotten an A on the exam and a B for the quarter. Because she had handed out our participation grades last Friday, nothing she could do today could change that.

Pawan and I discussed the Sanskrit test when the party got together for lunch. He was disappointed since he knew he had missed numerous questions, but he was already through with Sanskrit. He decided that instead of taking Sanskrit in high school, he would take French. I told him it was probably a good idea, but I was resigned to another year with Mrs. Poonam Singh since I wanted to take the Sanskrit literature course provided for juniors and seniors who had taken at least three years of Sanskrit *(and it also had a great future as history is my favorite subject, so they both align perfectly with each other)*. Everyone else appeared to think their test went well, and Priyanka was glad to have completed her band exam and performed her solo well enough that she believed she got an A. I was certain she did, since I had heard her play before and she was excellent.

My *'Last Physical Exam'* went as planned. I was pumped from outwitting Mrs. Poonam Singh, and despite not getting enough sleep the night before, I gave it my all in the test. In twelve minutes, I completed seven rounds of the track. The first 3/4 mile is the most difficult. I beat everyone and saved two long-distance track athletes who completed eight rounds in under twelve minutes. I've always been able to run long distances. If you asked me to run a sprint, I'd still be struggling to get out of the blocks when the first man crossed the finish line, but long distances were no problem for me. And, as I expected, the added advantage of bouncing growing breasts around the track, as well as nice bums in Physical shorts, didn't hurt and does give motivation.

For me, the last day of school was Wednesday. I only had 6 examinations from Monday to Wednesday since I only had one study hall. I liked how the school didn't require anyone who didn't have an exam to attend. On Wednesday, I had my first exam, which was Algebra. I breezed through the test, double-checked my work, then snatched up a book to pass the time. That was Mr. Ranjan Singh's style. Lunch was more of the same, but Pawan wasn't depressed since he'd decided to forget Mrs. Poonam Singh for good. I should have followed suit.

Ritvik appeared to be withdrawn, so I inquired as to what was bothering him.

"Nothing. I'm just trying to figure out certain things."

We hadn't seen each other in a month - Saturday was our typical hangout day, but I'd been busy for three days in a row *(two of which he couldn't know about).* I was at a loss for words. As a result, I changed the subject.

"Hey, cheer up!" I remarked. "The school chess competition is coming up next week."

"Yeah, that'll be great," he said with a smile.

I assumed he'd win the 10th-grade tournament and be in contention for the Jr. High championship. I'd be satisfied if I placed in the top five. He was better than me, but if he played poorly, I could beat him.

Yamini, on the other hand, was depressed, nearly to tears. She was aware that her visit to Delhi *(India)* was coming to an end and that she would be returning home.

"Don't be depressed!" I consoled her. "You have a lot of friends, we can write to each other, and who knows what the future holds. You'll be visiting all of your old pals and attending your old school. You'll also be able to see your dog. " I informed her.

Surprisingly, it was that dog that she missed the most. I preferred cats to dogs, but she had a Husky who she adored.

That made her grin. "I'm going to miss every single one of you. It's really difficult to go."

The bell rang exactly when she said it. "Thanks for remembering me," Yamini remarked as she glanced at me, stroked my hand, and smiled.

Her grin was one of my favorites. Her touch was wonderful. I wished for what may have been, but then I remembered Alisha's advice: simply be her friend. I didn't say anything but grin back as I walked away from the table.

Ch-12

The Miracle of Miracles...

The last exam of the year, Science, was not my favorite subject of the year as much as history, but it usually yielded good results.

I began with 'Atoms and Molecules,' an introductory chemistry course, then moved on to 'Machines,' 'Biology,' and finally, 'Electricity and Uses,' a beginning physics course, in the last quarter. This one was a no-brainer for me. All year, I hadn't missed a single point on homework or a quiz. I could sign the final, submit it in, and receive a B+. I rapidly went over the papers as they were handed out and almost burst out laughing. I only had two hours to complete this test. It would take 15 minutes to complete. And I'd be a natural at it.

I read it over, double-checked my work, and handed it in 20 minutes after class began. When I delivered it to Mr. Anil Pratap, he simply nodded, and I returned to my desk to read. A handful of kids gave me filthy glances, but Sonia Prajapati smiled at me, and I understood why. She handed in her test, turned around and poked her tongue out at me, and sat down two minutes later. She'd only made two mistakes all year. She earned the highest grades in the school, with all of her classes receiving straight A's. In science, on the other hand, I had her beat, and she was well aware of it.

"I intended to finish before you, but I got stuck on one question," Sonia stated as we were exiting the room after the exam concluded. I believe I did it correctly, but I had to redo it once. "See you next year!"

"Next time you thrust your tongue out at me, you better be prepared to use it!" I remarked, feeling confident and a touch frisky after my encounter with Alisha.

"Ashvini!" she exclaimed; her face flushed blazing red. She rolled her eyes. She was attractive, but she hadn't yet begun to mature. She walked away, huffing. I grinned. I'd gotten her so worked up that she didn't know what to do. With only one remark! Maybe next year I'll ask her to join me on a date.

I'm done for the year! I made my way to the bus, where I met Preeti and we continued our cricket conversation. We made arrangements to play some street cricket on Friday while all the kids were off because she was in 9th grade and wouldn't be at the

10th-grade class party. Since she moved in next door to us over two years ago, she and her brother Rakesh have been regulars at our street games.

On Thursday, I had the entire day free, but most of the group had examinations, so I decided to simply hang out at home, watch TV, and relax. Mom had a different plan. She handed me a list of duties as soon as I got up on Thursday *(I never slept late, always getting up with the sun)*.

"Aw, Mom, it's the first day of vacation!" I wailed.

"You're right, and this summer you're not going to sit around."

"Can you tell me what you're talking about? Next week is a chess competition, followed by two weeks of summer school and two weeks at Nainital. And, much like last year, it means two weeks of wandering through the woods and practicing basic survival skills! "

I was in the Disaster Management Program, and although certain aspects of it were enjoyable *(for example, the drill in which you carry gorgeous females on your shoulders and rescue them from disasters)*, the rest was tedious hell.

"Well, those are your responsibilities. If you want to go to the party tomorrow night, get moving. "

Threats are always present. There will be no more Sherlock Holmes, but there will be more Mogambo *(famous Indian movie villain)*.

I grabbed the hose and adapter and began power-washing the deck. As usual, pine needles were stuck between the boards, birds had made their usual mess, and there appeared to be a Coke spill. It wasn't difficult, but I was eager to read. I wanted to practice some chess openings and go through my new Super-Man comic book. Mom, on the other hand, had other plans, and I felt the sooner I finished, the better, even if it meant she'd load on more stuff.

I began working on the furnishings once the deck had been cleaned. There will undoubtedly be soda spills. Also, some sort of sauce. Anoop. It has to be that way. Last weekend, he and his pals *(all in sixth grade)* were out there. He was the one who caused the mess, and I was the one who had to clean it up. He's capable of accomplishing this. But instead, Mom assigned it to me while he ate breakfast at the kitchen table and watched something on the dining room's 21-inch TV. I simply shook my head and returned to my seat. After finishing the chairs, I moved on to laying mulch around the plants in front of the house. I got the wheelbarrow, went behind the garage, got two bags of mulch, loaded them up, and pushed the barrow around to the front of the house. I put on some gloves and split open the bags of mulch, spreading it about loosely before going to grab the rake to make it appear like I knew what she wanted.

Sheetal was waiting on the front step when I returned. My ten-year-old sister noticed, "Mom, got you slaving away again? She didn't even wait till the end of the school day. "

"Yeah, Sheetu, *(we call her fondly)," I replied dejectedly. "And, as usual, Anoop gets away with murder."

She agreed with a nod. She didn't, however, move to assist. This isn't surprising. She was the family's "Princess." Just ask my father about it. The point is, she didn't act like it was a big deal. She simply took advantage of the situation. I comprehended the circumstances and followed my destiny.

If I kept thinking about it, I'd become enraged, say something stupid to my mother, and miss out on Yamini's farewell party. On Monday, she was scheduled to fly to London. If my luck held, tomorrow would be the last time I saw her, for the rest of my life. I like to write, but I'm terrible at writing letters. Sheetal had a pen pal, so I figured I'd ask her about it. On the other hand, what would two ten-year-old girls speak about that I could utilize with Yamini? For the time being, I set that thought aside and went to get the lawnmower.

By midday, I had completed all of the outside tasks. I was relieved because it was going to be a hot day. The basement was next on the to-do list. We had table tennis and a TV room down there, as well as all of our toys. I had a feeling it was going to be a shambles. I hadn't gone down there with my pals in over a month, except for two Sundays ago when Om came over and we played table tennis. Anoop, on the other hand, was constantly down there with his pals. Oh, no! He's back.

I unlocked the game closet and began taking items out, placing them on the tennis table so I could reorganize them. The same could be said about the crates of green plastic army soldiers, tanks, and other war tools. I had a feeling about what would happen next, so I wasn't surprised when Anoop and his pals came down and told me I needed to relocate everything because they wanted to play table tennis. He knew mum had brought me down here to clean up the mess, and he knew he could now go complain to our mother that I did it simply to annoy him.

"I'm going to get very angry. Don't test my patience. I'm cleaning up, but I'm not moving anything, so you and your dumb buddies can play table tennis. You're the one who caused this mess, and I'm the one who has to clean it up. Get out of here."

I recognized the pattern. "Mom, Ashvini called my buddies stupid and won't allow us to play table tennis," he shouted to the mother.

"Get up here, Ashvini Surender Tyagi." For a long time, I had not heard *(my full name)* from my mother in this tone. This is becoming increasingly difficult for me. Yes, the pattern has been followed. As I pushed past Anoop up the stairwell, he grinned. I realized it was pointless to argue or whine, so I tried to be as rational as possible.

"Mom, I'm taking care of the duties you requested. I'll be done in an hour or so if he and his pals wait an hour or so. They'll ruin everything if I stop now, and I'll have to start over. "

"Well, they want to play table tennis, and you shouldn't have anything stacked on the table," she ordered me.

"Mom, they just want to play table tennis now because I am

cleaning up there and have put stuff on the table."

I was well aware that I was fighting a lost battle. It was much too significant a gathering. I gave in.

I got up and cleared the clutter from the table. I double-checked that nothing was near where they were going to be. They played one round of table tennis before deciding to walk outside. They did that intentionally to irritate me. Mom would never notice something like that. While I was straightening, I was enraged. I even covered the table and put the peddles away. I contacted Mom to check if I was done, since I didn't think Anoop and his mates would screw it up again.

Vacuuming the rugs was the last item on my to-do list. I pulled the vacuum out of the closet and carried it upstairs to vacuum the bedrooms and hallway. I needed a hose connection for the stairs, so I connected it up and finished them. The living room and family room come next, followed by the subterranean playroom. Anoop and his buddies hadn't returned to obstruct my progress, 'The Miracle of Miracles'. I stowed the vacuum, double-checked the list, informed Mom that I was finished, and went to my room. I locked the door, switched on the radio, and took out my new Super-Man comic book, which I had purchased as soon as it was released in 2002. After around three episodes of the comic, it occurred to me that I should also be preparing for a chess competition and that I should defeat Ritvik this time. As a result, I put down my comic and began reading one of my father's advanced chess instruction books, which he had given me on my 12th birthday. It was an easy book in some aspects, but I usually read it before a competition. I had a few other help books on chess, but that one seemed to constantly put me in a good mood and position during the matches.

I had no clue what my mother had planned for Friday, but I resolved right then and there to be as cheery and helpful as possible. It was simply too crucial for me to miss the celebration. It was a quiet dinner. Pasta with Italian sauce and fried eggs. As usual, it's drab. Ground eggs, tomato sauce, mushroom soup, and noodles are all that is needed. I made the decision that I needed to learn to cook. I didn't want to live the rest of my life that way *(I don't know what's happening to my mother's cooking nowadays)*. I went straight to my room after supper and didn't come out. I slept like a machine off for tonight and shall wake up tomorrow morning.

Ch-13

You Might Be Surprised...

It was a bright, beautiful, and pleasant Friday morning. The celebration was scheduled to be held on a wonderful day. I awoke, washed, and proceeded downstairs to eat breakfast. Freshly squeezed orange juice, egg omelettes, and homemade jam on toast. A little out of the ordinary. Mom intended to give me milk, but I asked *(begged)* for an apple instead. As I placed my dishes in the dishwasher, Mom remained silent, so I immediately retrieved a chess book, my cricket bat, and a ball from the garage and strolled down to the end of the block. Because I knew it would be at least an hour before the other kids arrived to play, I brought a book. I took a seat under an oak tree and began studying chess openings.

After twenty minutes, I noticed movement outside of the corner of my eye and looked up to see Preeti.

"Hey! I came out early since I saw you sitting out here. "

She was carrying her bat and another ball, and she was wearing a cap that made her appear stunning. This girl never fails to enthrall me with her antics. She is a sports maniac *(a rare trait in a female),* equally effective on the field, knowledgeable, with an athletic body and a contagious smile. What more did I overlook?

She's unorthodox, yet she's someone I'd want to date soon.

"Chess, huh?" she said, her gaze falling on the book's title.

"Yeah, I'm competing next week, and I'm hoping to place in the top five." That's something I've never done before. Ritvik Prakash is most likely to win. In tenth grade, he is the greatest. " I attempted to maintain a relaxed demeanor.

"I never learned to play. It looks overly convoluted. I'm going to stick to cricket." She replied with her left hand fixing her hat.

"Do I have it right? Or am I hallucinating? " I couldn't believe what I was hearing.

"Yeah! I've never played chess before. I suppose there's no shame in it. " She gave a response.

"There's no shame in it, but you're a sports encyclopedia." How could you do something like that to chess?" I attempted to pull her leg.

"Yeah, don't push it *(the topic);* put the book down, take the ball, and let's play catch. Perhaps the other kids will show up early. " She attempted to avoid the subject.

Because Preeti was the only girl who played with us, the "boys" were comfortable with her. Preeti and I began tossing the ball back and forth, and I suddenly spotted a cute girl beneath her curly perm. To be sure, she was a tomboy, but at 16, she was acquiring curves I hadn't seen before. I understood that my time with Alisha had made me hyper-sensitive to the feminine body and all of its pleasures. And now I dare to look for them. Preeti, on the other hand, was a true tomboy, so I doubted she'd be interested.

We tossed the ball back and forth for about 10 minutes until Rajat, Sourav, Ranjan, and Anmol arrived. While we waited for the other four players to arrive, they teamed up and began throwing balls back and forth. In the cul-de-sac, 5 to a side seemed to work nicely. We were still tossing ordinary cricket balls, but we were going to play with a softer ball. Windows were too pricey! Fortunately, there was an empty lot in the middle of the field, as well as half of the left and right fields. That was beneficial. The trees that provided some protection to the other houses did as well. We hadn't smashed any windows, but we were all getting older and needed to find a new spot to play where we could strike harder without causing any harm.

When the rest of the group came, Preeti and Anmol, the two greatest players at sixteen, took sides as usual. Preeti, like she normally did, picked me as her first choice. When I walked to stand next to her and remarked, "Can't resist me, I know," I showed off my newfound confidence. She giggled and slammed her fist into my shoulder. She didn't flush in the least. I wasn't surprised, though. She was a tomboy, so there was never anything sexual between her and any of the males *(we heard no rumors at least).* That was something I expected to change eventually. During the 9th and 10th grades, this constantly appeared to alter. She simply had a late start.

We were divided into teams and players. During the game, I made a couple of snider remarks to Preeti, who took them in stride. The folks who overheard gave me weird stares, but nothing was said. We won by a score of 12 runs. It was noon, and it was time for lunch. At 3:00 p.m., the celebration began. I gathered my belongings, said my goodbyes to everyone, and sprinted home.

Because she lived next door, Preeti was running beside me. She threw me a glance, chuckled, and walked away as I approached my house. I was curious as to what she was thinking. And it was this that made her chuckle. I was probably flirting with her. I'm curious if anyone else has done something similar. *(No one has ever dared maybe?)*

I ate lunch, showered, and changed into fresh shorts and a t-shirt. I sat in the family room, watching the news and weather report while waiting for Dad to pick me up and transport me to Lalita's place. Mom was out shopping, so she couldn't get in the way of my plans.

Dad arrived at 2:00 p.m., had a glass of water, and informed me that he was ready to leave where I was. I told him I wanted to depart at 2:30 p.m. since it would take around 20 minutes to go to Lalita's residence. Mrs. Deshpandey was bringing me home, I reminded him.

"Your mother instructed you to return home by 10:00 p.m."

"I know, Dad," I said with a sigh of relief.

I got out of the car, collected the snacks I had committed to bringing in, and headed over to the garden yard when we arrived. I stacked my belongings on one of the tables right inside the enormous barn doors and introduced myself to Lalita. I didn't put any of my newly acquired talents for girls to the test on her. In any way, shape, or form, she was uninterested in men. And she made it known to everyone. I wasn't going to argue with her about it and risk enraging her. There's no way.

Yamini and Ritvik came a few minutes later. They had been brought by her host mother. Mrs. Deshpandey planned to take all three of us home with her. I double-checked with Ritvik to make sure she was aware that I had to be in by 10:00 p.m. no matter what.

"Yes, she'll arrive at 9:30 p.m., and we'll leave you off before 10:00 p.m.," Ritvik assured me. "It's fine."

Yamini smiled and said, "Hi," before moving on to chat with Lalita.

"Man, I'm going to miss her," I stated after a brief conversation with Ritvik. "She's been a fantastic buddy and a lot of fun." He agreed without hesitation. "You should have gone for her while she was interested," I remarked.

"Nah, I don't think that would have worked."

I received a weird sense once more, but although being less naive than at the start of tenth grade, I had no idea what it was. I just let it go.

Yamini joined us with Kamini after Priyanka and Pawan arrived. Kamini had recently completed her first year and had come to the celebration to see Yamini. Normally, the class party was confined to just students from the same school and grade, but Lalita made an exception this time. Kamini was the polar opposite of Yamini in appearance, with dark hair and a wheatish complexion, yet both had stunning figures. The older males were quite interested in her. I had heard from Yamini that their next-door neighbor, a college student, was attempting to get her to go on a date, but she refused since she had a boyfriend.

We found an area at the rear of the barn, sat down, and put down an old blanket. "I'm going to miss all of you," Yamini remarked, looking at us all.

We all assured her that we'd miss her and that we'd write to her. I doubted it would happen, but I was willing to give it a go.

"What was the best thing that happened to you during your stay here?" I inquired.

"What do you mean, except from movies and ice cream?" she inquired, laughing.

Yamini was a big ice cream fan, and she informed us that the ice cream in London was great, and she liked it here as well.

"It has to be meeting all of you people, especially Ritvik and Ashvini," she concluded. "It's been a great year so far. I don't want to go, but I do want to visit my friends and return to my hometown. "

"As well as your dog."

"In particular, my puppy!"

The remainder of the night passed without any incident. Mrs. Deshpandey arrived on schedule, and Ritvik, Yamini, and I boarded the vehicle. Ritvik sat in the first row. I informed him that my family would be gone the next day and that I hoped he could come over. He said he may come over after his tennis lesson in the morning. I responded, "Great!" because everyone would be gone until at least supper time.

Yamini sat next to me the whole way, completely silent and only staring in my direction. I gave her a kind smile but said nothing. "Goodbye" was the only thing left to say.

When we arrived at my house, I opened the door to go and turned to say goodbye to Yamini. "I'll only be a minute," she remarked as she opened the door, surprising me.

She walked over to my side of the car and gave me a tearful look. I couldn't hold it in any longer, and a tear streamed down my cheek.

"I'll miss you," she murmured.

"I, too, will miss you."

She glanced at me, then walked up to me, wrapped her arms around me, and hugged me tightly. I hugged her back. After a brief moment of holding hands, I regretfully let go.

"I'll miss you, Yamini. I'll write, and I hope we'll run into each other again sometime."

"You might be surprised," she added, smiling through her tears. "It's impossible to predict what will happen."

She re-entered the vehicle and turned around. I stood there watching as they drove down the street, and Yamini vanished along with the car. I went into the house, checked to see whether Mom was awake, and went to bed. That night, I wept myself to sleep.

Ch-14

Are You Sure...

In June of 2002,

As usual, I awoke with the sun and went straight to the bathroom to shower. I was already missing Yamini, so I changed into the trousers and t-shirt she had given me. It seemed a little excessive for a Saturday, but it made me feel closer to her. I'd despise it if they wore out or didn't fit properly. I finished my dressing and walked downstairs for breakfast, which consisted of sugared porridge.

My father and brother were going to witness a model train display at the Rail Museum. My mom was putting my sister off to a friend's house for the night before coming to my grandmother's place, as she did most Saturdays. Nobody would arrive until after dinner. Ritvik would arrive at 10:00 a.m., as his tuition class was scheduled for 8:00 a.m. When my mother and father were not at home, he was the only one she would let inside the house. Despite the sadness, the day was shaping up to be a good one.

The 'OK' aspect was debunked by a thunderclap-at least in terms of the weather.

Dad got his coffee and half a grapefruit and added,

"Thunderstorms predicted for all day today."

"I wasn't planning on going out. Ritvik is coming over, and we're going to play chess and table tennis. The competition is next week."

As he sat down to eat, he remarked, "Have fun."

Mom kissed Dad as she entered with Sheetal. "Why are you dressed up?" she asked as she came to a halt.

"I simply felt like wearing the clothes Yamini gave me because Ritvik was coming over."

"Well, you're familiar with the regulations."

"I know, I know, Mom," I said.

She gave me a cold stare before heading out the door with Sheetal *(Mom being Hitler Mom).*

Dad completed his meal and proceeded to wake up Anoop, who had never gotten out of bed until being dragged out. Dad pounded on the door, announcing that he was going in ten minutes. With two minutes to spare, Anoop arrived dressed and ready to go. He walked into the kitchen and took a handful of cookies. As Dad walked out the door, the toaster beeped. Anoop snatched his food and dashed out the door.

"Bye, Ashvini," he said.

At the very least, Dad said goodbye to me.

"I'll see you tonight," I said.

Until Ritvik came, there wasn't much to do. I sat down with my books and a chessboard to remember various black replies to the Queen's Gambit opening, which was all the rage at the chess club at the time. This year, it seemed like everyone was playing some form of it. Today's topic was "Modern Variation." Heavy rain and howling wind were accompanied by thunder and lightning. A typical Delhi thunderstorm was caused by a western disturbance; however, it was a little early in the day at 8:00 a.m. I was listening to the weather on the radio. Normally, I mainly listened to the commentary of Indian cricket matches, but they featured frequent weather forecasts. All day it was supposed to rain on and off. I switched to a different channel.

I got up at 9:00 a.m., put my book down, and went outside to get some fresh air. I observed that the rain had subsided and that there was some sunshine. When the phone rang, I was standing in the kitchen. Ritvik was the name.

"Hey, I'm sorry, but I won't be able to make it today. Mom and Dad are on their way to my grandfather's place, and I am required to accompany them. If you wanted to, you could come."

He'd invited me before, but I'd never accepted his invitation.

"You know, I can't, since I don't have permission from my parents. My mom will certainly don't like it. I'm simply going to hang around here. I'm not in the mood to hang out with anyone right now."

He merely said a single syllable. This is a statement. This isn't a question. "Yamini."

"Yeah. Yamini. I'm already missing her. "

"I knew you wouldn't be able to go, but Mom insisted on asking." I apologize for making such a last-minute change, but my grandfather insisted. Have trust in Yamini; everything will work out."

He hung up after we said goodbye.

That was the extent of my plans for the day. I wanted a break from my chess book, so I walked downstairs and rehearsed my moves by putting both sides of the chess pieces on the chess board. I was improving and hadn't lost any of my pals in months *(except Ritvik)*. Granted, I was the only one with such folly, but I was brilliant at chess by myself *(who plays chess by themselves? Me)*. I went upstairs after approximately an hour of practicing.

It rained again, although not too severely this time. I went next door to see if Preeti was still alive *(just joking)*. I didn't think my parents would find out, and in the worst-case scenario, because they were out of town, we'd play a board game and then watch a cricket game *(or whatever sport was on)* on a sports channel. I dashed over to the next home and rang the doorbell. Preeti's mother came to the door.

"She's gone to her friend Anita's place," she replied.

I murmured, "Thanks anyhow, Mrs. Baghel," as I walked back to my house.

When I returned inside, sat down at the kitchen table, and began reading about the Slav Défense to the Queen's Gambit, a loud thunderclap and the doorbell rang nearly simultaneously. I was curious as to who it might be. Ritvik was in the company of his parents. Preeti was visiting a friend.

That meant there would most likely be strangers, as I was not expecting anyone, at least not in such stormy weather. I took a few steps to the front of the house and gazed out the window. In the driveway, there was a car I didn't recognize. I almost had a heart attack looking through the peephole. As I opened the door, my heart was hammering and my pulse was racing. Yamini was there wearing blue trousers and a blue fluffy t-shirt.

"Hello," she murmured timidly.

Then she turned around and waved at the automobile as it backed out of the driveway, leaving me speechless. I did nothing but stand there. I didn't know what to say.

"Aren't you going to welcome me in?" she asked.

I took a step back as she entered the house. I slammed the door behind me. I just stood there, staring. Finally, I was able to gather my wits.

"How did you end up here?"

"I need to see you again. I couldn't go without catching a glimpse of you. Because Kamini can't drive yet, I asked my host mother to drive me."

I was still stunned.

"How did you know I'd be here?"

"Ritvik. This morning, you were meeting up with him. You stated that last night in the car. He got out to say goodbye on the way home, and I requested him not to come over so I could. "

That explains Ritvik's spur-of-the-moment decision. I might have found something else to do if he had contacted me last night. I owed him money *(Thanks Bro!).* Even just spending a few hours with her would be worth more than anything I could ask for!

"Are we simply going to stand here?" she asked, a smile on her face.

"I'm sorry," I murmured, my face flushed. " All I can say is that I'm surprised to see you. Come on," I said while I escorted her into the living room.

I took a seat in my father's recliner. I didn't want her to get the wrong impression or feel uneasy. I didn't want to raise my expectations. She was going in two days, after all. She just sat on the couch, staring at me. I couldn't think of anything to say. I'd be content to simply sit and stare at her for a few hours.

That prompted me to inquire, "How long will you be staying?"

She narrated, "Kamini and her mum will be returning about 4:30 p.m. Your parents should be home about 5:00 p.m., according to Ritvik."

I was curious as to what she had in mind.

"Would you want anything to drink?" I inquired *(I sounded like a bartender).*

"Sure, just a glass of water," she replied, smiling.

I got up, went to the kitchen, and fetched her some water, with a few ice cubes thrown in for good measure. I brought some apple juice for myself.

The storm came up again as I stepped back into the family room. The thunder made the panes shiver. She pulled the glass from my grip and drank from it.

"Thanks."

"Sure."

I sat down in the recliner once again. I cranked up the radio's volume. I reasoned that a little music wouldn't hurt. Imagine my amazement when **Tip-Tip Barsa Paani, Paani Ne Aag Lagayi** was the first song that aired... (*A Famous Hindi Song From Mohra Movie, Starring Sizzling Ravina Tandon and Dashing Akshay Kumar*).

"Perfect!" Yamini said, laughing.

I gave her a kind grin. She returned the smile. (*English and Hindi Meanings Mentioned in the song*)

Tip-Tip, Barsa Paani,

(Drop Drop Water Rained)

(*टिप-टिप बरसा पानी !*)

Tip-Tip Barsa Paani, Paani Ne Aag Lagayi,

(Drop by Drop, Water Rained, Water Caught Fire)

(*टिप-टिप बरसा पानी, पानी ने आग लगाई !*)

Aag Lagi Dil Me To, Dil Ko Teri Yaad Aayi,

(There Was A Fire In My Heart, My Heart Remembered You)

(*आग लगी दिल में तो, दिल को तेरी याद आई !!*)

Teri Yaad Aayi To, Jal Utha Mera Bheega Badan,

(If I remember you, my wet body got burnt)

(*तेरी याद आई तो, जल उठा मेरा भीगा बदन !*)

Ab Tu Hi Batao Sajan, Main Kya Karun...

(Now you tell Me My Lover, What Should I Do?)

(अब तू ही बताओ सजन, मैं क्या करूँ!!)

The song, on the other hand, was sensual and well suited to our circumstances. And it wasn't a break-up song, as far as I knew. We weren't splitting up since we'd never been together in the first place, but she was going. It may, I suppose, lead to something else. I'm crossing my fingers.

"I'm going on Monday morning, as you know. And I needed to ask you a question."

"Sure. Anything."

"Do you recall how I contacted you three weeks ago after my going away party? And inquired as to who she was?"

"You know I can't tell you," I said. "I shouldn't have even confessed anything happened, but I couldn't tell you the truth."

"I understand. But I was curious as to what had happened. How did it happen? You never mentioned any females. You've never spoken to me." Her eyes were getting bigger and bigger, her lips moving out of curiosity. She wanted to know everything.

I thought about what I should say. Is it really necessary for me to say anything? I had to be cautious, even though she was going on Monday. Even the stupidity of a clue might spell disaster *(And I am the Master of Stupids)*.

"It wasn't anything I expected to happen. Someone I'd known for a while but who didn't attend our school wanted to join me. I'm a male. I wasn't sure what I was going to say. 'No'?" Nervously, I laughed.

"No, I wouldn't expect you to," she said with a smile. "And I still find it amusing that the 'Simple London Girl' is a virgin but you aren't. Would you be willing to tell me what you did? I'm intrigued. Tell me every single piece of it."

This is risky territory. And I had no idea why she was inquiring.

I responded calmly, "We did all the normal stuff. I've seen her a few times, but I believe it's over. Like a long-term relationship, it wasn't going to work out. But I wouldn't change it for anything. I wasn't-over heels in love with her, but I had strong sentiments for her. In the end, I was disappointed, but I suppose she was correct."

It's up to Yamini to predict correctly once more. "An elderly woman," she jumped on and I was bemused. "Doesn't go to our school. I bet she doesn't go to a high school. College girl? Much older?" She fired bullets from her mouth and I was in the thick of it now.

"Please, Yamini," I begged, but I couldn't persuade her.

She was going to get me to provide more information than I should have. But I couldn't help myself.

"She's 25+," I told her. "Someone I met a few years ago, although she was unaware of it due to those circumstances." We met a month ago, and I was dressed in that clothing. She mistook me for someone older, and..."

"You look eighteen or nineteen when you wear those," Yamini said.

"... she invited me to her house, and I suppose you could say she seduced me. Even though I informed her I was only sixteen, she went ahead and did it anyhow. You can't tell anyone, though. We'd both get into trouble, and she'd be in danger. *(I told her half-truth and half-fiction.)*"

"I'm not going to inform anyone," she said in an affirmative tone. "I was merely curious as to how my friend moved from being timid and scared around females to being confident; why he was so joyful for two weeks... and then so depressed for another week."

She got attention! I believed I'd managed to conceal it. My emotions, I suppose, deceived me.

She went on to say, "It was your eyes that gave you away. I could tell you were upset about something deep down within. I assumed it was because I was leaving, but I wasn't sure. I knew how much you'd missed me last night, and I was certain it wasn't the same thing. That's one of the reasons I begged Ritvik to go so I could come here. I was curious as to what was going on. You weren't telling me what you were going through."

"I couldn't do it. What could I possibly say? Anything I said had the potential to bring so much pain to someone who gave me so much pleasure. I had no intention of doing it. I shouldn't even be discussing it right now. But I'm confident you won't say anything."

"Thank you," she murmured with a big smile on her face. "Thank you very much. It means a lot to me that you trust me."

I couldn't think of anything to say, so I just nodded as she stared at me.

"Was it that good?"

"It was," I answered, a faint smile on my face. "Fortunately, she understood just what to do, which prevented me from humiliating myself or making a total fool of myself. It was incredible. I always imagined myself fumbling about in the back of a car or trying to locate a hiding spot and dashing through it. Those were the tales I was always told. Instead, it was leisurely, in a comfortable bed, and with a knowledgeable partner. I wouldn't exchange it for anything." I started lying more and more since I was now having fun teasing her.

She simply sat and stared at me. I couldn't read her emotions as well as she could read mine, but there was something wrong. I wanted to be able to read females one day, but I wasn't expecting it. My father, who was 50+ at the time, was fond of declaring that no one had ever figured out women. I knew girls were perplexing, but I believed I'd figure it out when I grew older. But I wasn't so sure anymore. Perhaps Dad was correct.

She finished her water and set the glass on the table. The storm had passed, and there was a ray of sunshine.

"Let's go outside for a few minutes in between the rainstorms," she suggested as she stood up.

We stepped out the back door onto the terrace once I woke up. Because of the rain, the fragrance of the forests behind our house was overwhelming. It was, however, pretty tranquil. "It's wonderful," she commented as we stood there staring at the trees. It's unusual to have a perspective like this, and it's all fascinating. I'm not capable of doing it daily as you are."

I answered, "Yeah, it's lovely."

For almost five minutes, we stood there.

"Can I ask you something else, Ashvini?"

"Of course," I affirmed.

"Do you believe we'll cross paths again?"

"Well, after yesterday, I didn't think so, but you came up here today after indicating I might be shocked." I was certainly one of them. "Did you already have it planned?"

"No, but after saying that, I decided to try if I could make it happen when I got back in the car. That is exactly what I did. Ritvik was eager to lend a hand. I was a little anxious about my host mother, but she was OK."

"You were the one who made it happen. So, I think my response is yes, we'll meet up again. I'm not sure where we'll go or when we'll get there, but we'll get there. Maybe I'll visit London eventually."

"Really?" She smiled again, that killer smile, and said, "Perhaps I should teach you some skills, then," with a twinkle in her eye.

"Oh? You have taught me things. Can you tell me what you want me to teach right now?"

"Just a phrase," she remarked as she turned to return home. She patted the cushion next to her as she sat on the couch. I took a seat, taking care not to go too close. "I want you to say to me, I love you. Come on repeat after me," she ordered.

"Do you want me to say it?"

She gave a hesitant laugh. "Well, you should respectfully ask if I would want to make love to you, and I will answer yes, I would."

My mouth hung wide, and I found myself dumbfounded once

more. This appeared to be a pattern - girls, not women, tended to have the same impact on me. "Are you taunting me again?" I said quietly after regaining some calm.

"No, Ashvini, I'm not joking. It's difficult, but I'm confident that's what I want. I was terrified that something would happen that would kill our friendship. Or that it would be so bad that we would come to regret it. However, you've changed a lot in the previous several weeks. I believe you can manage this at this point. And I'm confident that I can as well."

"Wait, you didn't want to have love with me before when we were both virgins?" She asked ferociously.

"Wait, you didn't want to have love with me before, but now you do? I'm not sure what you're talking about. What about Ritvik, for example? How did it go with the rejection? You were more into him than me." I snapped.

She appeared to be on the verge of crying. I guess she felt I was rejecting her, but I was in shock for the second time that day and couldn't think straight. "No!" she said angrily. "I've always liked you, but I was terrified. I thought it would be enjoyable to spend out with Ritvik since he seemed safer, but I never imagined it would lead to anything meaningful. I was scared we'd start something, and then I'd have to go, and it'd be over. I was concerned we'd make a shambles and lose touch. I was frightened of being in a situation where I didn't know what to do. I believe your vision of the sexually liberated British girl with all the skills and answers from birth is now a thing of the past."

Her anxiety returned to her face after a fleeting grin at her comments. ***"Are you sure you don't want to?"***

Ch-15

Mother Swear, I Haven't...

Was it something I wanted to do? Was she joking? In the worst possible manner, I wanted to. But, once again, I was going to jump right into something and finish it awkwardly. How I ruined things with Alisha is still fresh in my memory. But it's not the same. This one offered a variety of options. She would, however, be gone on Monday. 4100+ miles away, only letters will be accepted. And, for the time being, traveling to London was a pipe dream. As I pondered what to do, the tiny head instructed the large head what to do, and this became a pattern in my life. And this time, the small head had the heart. I simply looked at her and responded, "Yes."

The magic was shattered as the phone continued to ring.

I stood up to respond. It was Dad, who was on his way to see my mother after the train show with Anoop. He was going to Grandma's for supper, and he wanted to make sure I knew so I could prepare food instead of waiting for them. They'd all return home around 9:00 p.m. If they were going to be late, he'd call. "No problem," I answered as I hung up the phone.

"My father - they won't be home until at least 9:00 p.m.," I told her.

With a large smile on her face, she grabbed the phone and dialled Kamini's number, telling her that instead of coming at 4:00 p.m. with mum, they should come at 8:00 p.m., received confirmation, and hung up the phone. "Show me your room," she added as she turned to face me.

I got up from my seat, took her hand in mine and walked her upstairs to my room. No girl had been here in a long time except Sheetal, because having girls in my room was a no-no with my mother. No one has ever come close to doing this. Thankfully, I kept my room tidy and clean. There are no clothes on the floor or anything like that. But there was one thing I had forgotten: 'Goofy Teddy Bear' was smack dab in the middle of my bed.

My plush animal, *'Goofy Teddy Bear'*, has been with me since I was six months old. It was some sort of bonus from a bank that my parents used. Yamini looked around the room and noticed my photos with some of India's greatest cricketers, including Sachin Tendulkar, Rahul Dravid, Sourav Ganguly, and my personal favourite, VVS Laxman. Many different automobile and motorcycle models, as well as a replica of the warship INS Vikrant and a large poster of Titanic star Kate Winslet. My favourite photo is with India's rocket scientist, Dr APJ Abdul Kalam (*fondly called Missile Man of India*).

"A stuffed Teddy Bear?" she said, chuckling as she gazed at the bed. "Seriously?"

"Yeah! That's something I've had for a long time. I don't sleep with it, but he does spend the day in my bed."

I thought that could have ruined the mood.

"Wow, that's adorable!"

I shut the door even though no one was home. I then drew the shade down almost all the way. As it was still pouring, there wasn't much light, but the odd flash of lightning projected an eerie glow into the room. Because my standing light had a dimmer control, I turned it halfway on. Even though she had started it, I was a little hesitant. I was both certain and uncertain. It was a dream come true for me, but I was terrified I'd mess it up. That I'd sabotage the occasion. She wasn't going to like it.

Let me now take you inside a sixteen-year-old's head. In such a setting, what's going on?

Contraception is a method of birth control. I didn't have any condoms and had no idea where I might acquire any because the nearest drug shop was a few miles away. I wasn't sure they'd sell them to me even then. I assumed that children could purchase them, but I had never done so. A million thoughts ran through my head.

I must have had a hazy expression on my face. Yamini walked over to me, grabbed my hands in hers, and softly kissed me on the lips without saying anything. She sat on the edge of the bed after a brief but exhilarating kiss. I was about to say something when she put her finger to my lips and said gently and shyly.

"Aside from kissing, I've never done much. I did let one boy touch me on my clothing once. Of course, I've seen males naked in the sauna, but I've never seen anything more. I've had some feelings for the lads, as well as some strange physical reactions, but I've never been with a boy to that level, you know? I visited my host mother's room today and took one of her pills *(birth control)*. My mother warned me not to trust men because they would get me pregnant if I started experimenting, and she didn't believe they could be trusted to be responsible. I'm frightened and shaking, but I'm confident that this is something I want to accomplish. Will you please make love to me?" She grabbed my collar and asked.

How could I possibly say no to that? But I was so eager that I believed my jeans were going to rip. I was terrified that I wouldn't be able to make it worthwhile for her. Two Saturdays with Alisha made up my whole experience, which was incomplete. And I've boasted to Yamini about how I've been with an older lady and have done all that's expected of me *(Mother swear, I haven't)*. Now it was up to me to take command. With a sweet little girl who was counting on me to make her first time a memorable one. What if I let her down? What if it all went wrong? A thousand images flashed over my head. Many of them are awful, but a select number are exceptional. And what should I say? I couldn't afford to be late since she was waiting for me.

All I said was "Yamini..."

I grabbed her hands in mine and helped her to her feet. I drew her into a close embrace. I was sure she could feel my hand on her leg. She wrapped her arms around me and embraced me passionately. But I sensed her averting her gaze from the bulge in my trousers. I chalked it up to nerves and inexperience but hoped it wasn't a hint of hesitancy or fear that may sway her decision.

If that happened, I would honour her wishes. I comprehended that "no" means "no." I'd simply go easy on it and see what happens. There was no urgency because we had a long time until she was taken up.

I ran my hands down her back, rubbing against the soft fuzzy fabric of her clothing. I was shocked she wore it on such a hot day, but then I realised it made sense with the air conditioning on in the home. Come to think of it, I was also wearing long sleeves. She drew back slightly, making only the tiniest touch between her tiny, firm breasts and mine, and looked me in the eyes.

I understood exactly what she wanted and pressed my lips to hers. Our tongues met for the first time when she sighed softly and opened her lips. It felt like I had been struck by lightning. A flash of lightning and a crash of thunder flooded the room with a yellowish hue, and the glass was shattered. Our tongues twirled around one another, and our bodies melted into one. She wasn't backing away from me anymore, and the closeness was driving me insane. This is the first time I've ever felt like this *(Incredible).*

I let my hands fall on her buttocks and drew her closer to me. Things were moving correctly, and I was careful not to move too much and destroy everything and humiliate myself. Our kisses became increasingly passionate, even desperate. Mouths and tongues brushed up against one other with vigour. Her hands also made their way to my body. I was near to heaven with her body fitted to mine. I slid one hand to her hip, then up her side, just touching the side of her breast with the other. And....

The doorbell rang...

Ch-16

When Your Hormones Do The Talking...

We stopped kissing and looked at each other in disbelief. And then the doorbell rang again. This time, for a longer period of time.

"Ashvini! There's a knock at the door," Yamini yelled at me while I stood there as numb as I could be.

This can't possibly be my parents, let alone my mother. She can't possibly be. Alternatively, Ritvik may be at the door, pranking us in the middle of... *(you know...)* In my head, a lot of things were going on. For the third time, the bell rang.

"Ashvini, will you open the door or will you not?" Yamini yelled after smacking me, and I snapped back to reality.

"Yes, I'm heading down. Attach the video game here and attempt to play it. Begin with a two-player game. " At our house, I attempted to find an escape route with Yamini's presence in my room.

My mother knew Yamini, and if things went out of hand, I'd tell her that Yamini had come to say her final goodbyes before leaving. Then I served her sandwiches and juice, the rain started, and we started playing video games to pass the time. Bingo! This is a fantastic trick.

I was both startled and dismayed when I looked through the peephole. I answered the door dejectedly.

"Hello, Ashvini! You did take a long time to open the door? What were you up to, champ? " Shilpa, my maternal aunt, barraged me with questions as she entered our living room.

"I... Aunt Shilpa, I was playing video games with a friend. Please accept my apologies for the delay." I lowered my head.

"Oh, my poor baby, don't be depressed. Come in and hug me. You have matured. You were a ten-year-old munchkin peeing on his bed the last time I saw you." She kissed my left cheek as well.

Meet Shilpa, my maternal aunt. She is a 21st-century fun-loving, free-flowing, don't give a crap attitude gal. She goes around the globe from one end to the other. She can't stay anywhere for more than three weeks at a time. She is a painter pursuing her master's degree, and numerous institutions throughout the world have offered her a permanent position to work, which she accepts but as a freelancer. People from all around the world fund her excursions, pay her handsomely, and allow her to live her life to the utmost.

She's presumably in her thirties, stunning and superb at communication skills. If you are conversing with her, she will take your heart without telling you. She is a nomadic wanderer who lives alone. I had the impression that she was not from my maternal family and that my maternal grandparents must have adopted her. Her likeness to my mother's features, though, is the only reason anyone could think she is from Earth. What I always wanted was to become like her, and live my life my way. I don't know how much time I take to live such a life.

"Your mother told me yesterday that there would be no one else in the home but you. And I'm pleased it occurred in the same way because Mom would have reprimanded me every time if it hadn't. Ashvini, you're not going to give me a lecture, are you?" She inquired as she retrieved the spaghetti and drink from the refrigerator.

"Why would I...?" I didn't finish my sentence.

"Exactly! What right do you have to lecture me? I'm twice your age and have far more life experience than you. I am the one who should be interrogating you. Why did you wait so long to open the door? Whom are you playing games with? Your mother advised me that until she returns, none of your friends should be permitted to see you at home." And she continued to speak incessantly.

"I was... I was playing..." I was on the verge of passing out. My Aunt was no less psycho than my mother.

"We were playing together." Yamini interfered and somehow rescued me.

"Well... Well... Well... Who is this young lady?" she asked.

"Aunt Shilpa, her name is Yamini, and she is a friend of mine. She is moving back to London now that school has ended, so she was visiting every friend's house to say goodbye. Then I offered her some sandwiches and a drink, and then it started raining, so we went into my room and started playing video games." Rather than my mum, I practiced my planned speech in front of Aunt Shilpa.

"I assumed she was your girlfriend, and you were both doing things that teens your age are supposed to do." She laughed.

"No... no... we're just pals, and we never... no, we didn't" I freaked out and messed around, doing what I do best: ruining things.

Yamini shifted her gaze to me.

"Oh. What a pity. You're both intended to look attractive together," Shilpa, my aunt, yanked my leg.

"Mam, we're close friends right now, and we don't know what the future holds for us. We like each other's company, and now that I'm returning to London, I'm hoping I won't find anybody else's company to be better than his." Yamini was able to match fire with fire.

"I hope I haven't interrupted you if you were in the middle of anything important, you beauty? You are free to continue. Just act as though I'm not here." My aunt responded with a jab at Yamini.

Yamini was rendered speechless. A pin-drop stillness fell over the room. I need to step in, and I need to do it quickly.

"Aunt Shilpa, what brought you to Delhi so unexpectedly? You were in Paris the last time I heard from you, so ten days ago?" I tried to steer the conversation away from the subject.

"I was present. And the previous three days had been spent in London. And in fifteen days, I'll be in Shanghai. That's how I live." She responded.

"However, there must be some exceptional cause or event?" I inquired once more.

"Yes, here in Delhi, there is an organization for orphan children. They're holding a charity event, and I'm here to auction off my paintings to the highest bidders, with the proceeds going to the orphanage. That is the cause of the unique event." She had informed me.

Hearing this, Yamini felt a little guilty about her (Aunt Shilpa) unexpected entry into this house. She wanted to know more about her immediately, but she couldn't talk for reasons best known to her.

"That's very appreciable, Aunt Shilpa. Have you always been in this charity thing or to it your first time?" I inquired.

"I've been doing charitable work since I was twelve years old. I used to volunteer in the community on Sundays while I was in school. Then I was joined by a couple of my buddies. It grew into a group of thirty or forty kids. Then we began collecting donations for others in our neighborhood who were in need (elderly and widows). We also gathered money for youngsters who used to beg at traffic lights to fulfill their right to education. In college, I was elected president of the Student Union and encouraged students to participate and contribute more. My efforts were noted, and I was invited to work with the United Nations in Africa. And since then, I've seen so much in this world that has to be addressed. And I make every effort to tell others about it. That's how I live." In front of us, she encapsulated her entire existence.

Aunt Shilpa had both of us in awe. I had never seen her in such a light before. She was a free bird to me, living her life according to her own set of rules, but today I met the real Aunt Shilpa. We inquired about her travels to Africa and other countries. She took us on all of her journeys. She's more of a spell-caster; the way she described her trips was like watching a movie unfold in front of our eyes. We *(Yamini and I)* were dancing to her tracks because her lyrics were magical. As she was writing a novel, she got a hint for the following narrative at the conclusion of each one. It always seemed to end, but she always left us hanging on the precipice, and by going on to the next narrative, she always became our rescue. So did the clock; it was about 15 past four o'clock.

"I wish I could join you after graduation, Aunt Shilpa. Your philanthropic activities have greatly inspired me, and I, too, want to contribute to our nation in such a way that I may aid the poor without becoming greedy." Yamini talked about her plans for the future.

"There's no need to wait for graduation. You may begin with simple steps. Begin on your street, in your neighborhood, and your community. Help stray animals by providing food and animal care *(first aid)*. People should be made aware of the situation. Organize awareness drives at least twice a month. Make sure that your cause attracts a growing number of volunteers. There are several options. Begin with a modest step; it doesn't have to be big, but it should be consistent. Then, one day, your valiant efforts will contribute to our country's and humanity's prosperity. " Aunt Shilpa gave Yamini an entire speech.

"Aunt Shilpa, may I hug you?" Yamini had made a request.

"Of course, you do!"

Aunt Shilpa murmured something in Yamini's ear as they held each other. Yamini gazed at her in surprise, then at me, before laughing. Even though I was standing so close to them, I couldn't hear what they were saying.

The clouds parted, allowing sunshine to flood the room.

"Ashvini! Don't you two need some time together *(or play video games)?* It would also be fantastic if you two could make some room for me. As I've just returned after a lengthy journey. Then I'd take a bath and rest." Aunt Shilpa was the one who dragged my leg there.

"Yes… Yes, we must… We have no choice but to play video games." I became agitated once more. What the heck was going on with me? I've never panicked as much as I did today in my whole life.

We went upstairs to my room after Aunt Shilpa relocated to the guest room.

"I think I should contact my host mother to pick me up now, Ashvini," Yamini started abruptly.

"However, we were in the midst of..." I didn't finish my sentence.

"Yes, if something didn't happen today, it didn't have to happen today. I'm the type of person that believes in the power of symbols. God sends us messages; if He is preventing you from doing anything, it is because it was not His desire. Maybe he'll decide for you at a later date." Yamini's religious side was on display.

"Permit me to express my admiration for you! You're a fantastic kisser, and I had a lot of fun with you at that time. You made me feel like a princess, and I was in a different world at the time." She expressed her emotions.

I couldn't tell which way the talk was heading. I, on the other hand, was following her lead.

"I wanted to visit you again before I left, which I did today *(with a whole new perspective).* Until the bell sounded, one thing led to another and practically everything. I thank Aunt Shilpa for bringing me back to reality and recognizing that *'You are the love of my life.'* And we were ready to wreck everything for ourselves *When Your Hormones Do The Talking*." She started to feel emotional.

"I'll keep an eye out for you. I'll wait for you. I'll remain in touch, write to you frequently, and do my best to visit you around the holidays. I don't have any expectations of you, but I hope you'll be patient with me, you will wait for me too." She concluded.

"Yeah sure," I said, and the words stuck in my mouth.

She hugged me and said goodbye.

"What was it that Aunt Shilpa murmured in your ear?" I inquired.

"She said, - play video games or wrestle about, but never let any male bite your bottom lip," Yamini answered and left for her host parent's home.

What future beholds for Yamini and Ashvini, do stick around to find out in the upcoming second part of *Intense Desires Series- The Darkest of Hours...* Till then, be safe, care for your loved ones and please know us about your views @ hbkhilady@gmail.com or instagram.com/khilady_day_out/

ABOUT THE AUTHOR

Hanish Bhardwaj Khilady

Author | Life Coach | Numerologist | Content Creator | Script Writer | Screen Play Writer | Co-Founder at Phoenixate Tutorials

www.ingramcontent.com/pod-product-compliance
Lightning Source LLC
Chambersburg PA
CBHW061326120726
48001CB00002B/718